A Regency Christmas

by

Susan Payne

An Anthology

This is a work of fiction. Names, characters, places, and incidents are either the product of the author's imagination or are used fictitiously, and any resemblance to actual persons living or dead, business establishments, events, or locales, is entirely coincidental.

A Regency Christmas

COPYRIGHT © 2020 by Susan Kay Payne

The Wild Rose Press, Inc.
PO Box 708
Adams Basin, NY 14410-0708
Visit us at www.thewildrosepress.com

Publishing History
First Bouquet Rose Edition, 2020
Trade Paperback ISBN 978-1-5092-3313-7
Digital ISBN 978-1-5092-3314-4

Published in the United States of America

Dedication

For my darling daughter Heather Lynn whose most favorite time of year was Christmas. May she always have the joy and love of the season surround her.

Table of Contents

A Regency Christmas Story

CHAPTER ONE

"Oh Christopher, how could you do such a thing? How am I to explain to the shopkeepers they must wait yet again?" Penny couldn't understand how grown men expected gambling debts to be paid within days while hardworking vendors and tradesmen were expected to wait sometimes months. She tried to make sure their expenses were covered by the small annuity her father left them, but she had not considered her brother's needs as he grew into manhood. Dress clothes, hackney fees, and costs of evening entertainments were more than her monthly household budget. She looked at his sandy colored hair as he kept his brown-eyed gaze fastened to the carpet unable to lift them to meet hers. A sure sign he wanted to argue.

"You could start working for a fee rather than volunteering at that blasted children's school." He sounded angry. "There are jobs out there for that lot if they would stop whining to soft-hearted people like yourself. I mean, they made do before you came and they will do just as well without you."

Why would he think she should abandon their father's work? Her younger brother knew how important their father thought these schools were for the children left homeless and often parentless as well.

"They do not do 'as well' without people like me. I have been working with these children for eight years, ten if you count the years Father took me with him to help the little ones learn to read." She hated this argument which had been coming up more and more often in their conversations recently. Even if she did ask for a wage, the school couldn't afford much and certainly nowhere near the amount of money her brother seemed to need.

"Then I think you've done your fair share. It's time to let other do-gooders work for free while you find a position that would pay what you're worth." He grasped her hand to make sure she knew he was sincere. "You know you are wasting yourself trying to help those street urchins."

She was pleased he thought her worth being paid but saddened at his lack of charitable thoughts. So different from their parents, she sometimes wondered what turned her towards helping those with less while Christopher leaned so far in the other direction. "I think if you do not purchase any more clothes and walk to your club rather than hire a hackney each time…."

His face was a comic mask of a man insulted. "No one arrives at his club on foot. That's for servants and commoners!"

"And you are a commoner, no matter how much you like to flaunt your relationship to a viscount. You know Viscount Varley wouldn't recognize you if he passed you on the street nor you him, I imagine. I know I wouldn't."

"It so happens I ran into him a few months ago. We had a very friendly chat about horses at Tattersalls."

"Did he know to whom he was speaking? I mean did he recognize you?" She had to question her brother on this since he hadn't mentioned the meeting before now.

"Not at first. I had to prod his memory a little as you know the relationship is a tad stretched, but he did nod to me when our paths crossed a while later." Her brother wasn't looking at her which was a clear sign he wasn't being honest with her over what had happened or he didn't want her to know what had happened.

"I suppose you were there for an auction. One of your friends looking into buying a horse?" She wouldn't press him on his need to feel connection to a relative so far removed the man barely knew of their existence.

"As a matter of fact, I put in a bid." He shot his cuffs, giving him a reason not to see her shocked expression.

"Christopher! What were you thinking? Not only is there no money to purchase a horse, we also do not have the funds to maintain a horse in town. The food and stable rental alone would destitute us."

"Calm down, I merely bid on the nag. I knew there was no way it would go for the first bid or two. I simply wanted to see what it would feel like to place a bid, then appear as if I had thought better of it and started looking over the next few horses coming up for bid. I wanted to see what it felt like to seem to be able to buy a horse."

Penny's heart broke for her brother as he sounded like the same twelve-year-old boy who dropped his bowl of ice outside of Gunter's. It was a once in a summer treat and in his exuberance of receiving the dish, Christopher tripped as most young boys do who haven't gotten used to having longer legs and bigger feet. As he stood looking at the melting dessert, his bottom lip began to quiver. Penny shoved her dish into his hand saying, "Take mine. I find it too cold on my tongue." Her brother accepted the dish and more carefully walked across the street to the park and ate it while talking to some other boys he found there.

She had the same tightness in her chest every time she had to deny him something he wanted. He may have much more than those children she taught in the free-school, but she knew he felt the same need and yearning for those things just out of his reach.

"I'm glad you realized we can't afford a horse at this time, but perhaps we can see to having the funds to rent one to ride in Hyde Park."

Once more his expression showed one of aghast. "I would rather be caught walking shirtless down Piccadilly Road than be seen on a rented hack. What can you be thinking, Penny?"

"I thought it was the act of riding you sought, not being seen preening on an animal you can't afford." Her patience was up. He had succeeded in diverting her attention away from the fact he not only over-spent, but the precious funds they had had been squandered on gambling. How selfish of him to put his entertainment ahead of their needs.

He looked stunned, as if she had slapped him, but soon recovered shrugging his shoulders. "You needn't worry about it, Sis. I have it under control. I merely mentioned it in case you were expecting a Christmas present this year. I fear I will not have the funds." Once more he shot his cuffs and crossed the room to retrieve his silver topped walking cane. "I won't be in for supper. Enjoy your evening."

She watched out the window as he let himself out now wearing his great coat and top hat. He looked so handsome her anger melted away. She needed to remember he was much younger than her when they lost their parents. Penny was sure her father would have set him to rights if he had lived longer, but he succumbed to a fever raging through the London slums just as one had taken her mother two years earlier.

No one could say the Cooper family hadn't paid their dues. Helping the underprivileged had cost them most of their money, much of their time, and both her parents. Perhaps Christopher was right in saying enough was enough. She walked toward the balls of yarn ready to be knit into scarves and socks for those less fortunate and sat in her usual spot close to the unlit fire. The sun was shining, at least, which meant a savings on both heat and candles. Picking up the scarf already underway, she tucked the yarn over her fingers and began to knit.

CHAPTER TWO

A rapping of the knocker against the front door had Penny rushing to answer it. Some internal sense forewarned her it wasn't the usual tradesmen, for they normally went around back and spoke to Dora, even about past due accounts. Possibly this was a bill collector hired by one of their many creditors. She schooled her face to accept whatever was outside the wide wooden door.

"May I help you?" She was glad she had taken a moment to prepare herself for anything for the tall gentleman standing there appeared as surprised as she felt as he stared at her well past politeness.

He was a gentleman and surely not a bill collector which had Penny's heart beat slowing to normal or as normal as she could make it considering the attractiveness of the man in front of her. His attire was of the finest quality and one her brother would have envied even if a little conservative for Christopher's taste. This man was tall and slim but broad across the shoulders. Piercing grey eyes under wide brows matching the dark hair cut short leaving the sideburns low on his cheeks. He also must employ a valet since his cravat was snowy white and tied perfectly with a diamond stickpin peeking through the intricate folds. His gloved hands held an ornate silver walking stick which he must have used on her door. She hoped it hadn't left any dents but was too mesmerized by the aristocratic face with its straight nose, deep-set eyes and high cheekbones to check. The intensity of his appraisal of her was taking the same amount of time as hers did of him.

She repeated, "May I help you?" to break the spell.

He blinked and then a smile she thought he hadn't meant to present crossed his sensual lips. "I have come to speak with Mister Christopher Cooper. Is he at home?"

She knew that the door would have been answered by a butler or at least a footman even in this part of town and felt herself blush as she took on that position informing the caller the truth. "I am afraid Mister Cooper is not at home, sir. Would you care to leave a card?" There she completed her part relatively unscathed. Now he could pass her a card or not and then leave.

It was but a moment when he said, "Then I find I must speak to his business manager."

That flummoxed her. Plus, if this man was here for Christopher's business manager, she was the one he wanted to speak with since she controlled all funds from the annuity. "Perhaps you should come in, sir." She stepped back opening the door wider allowing precious heat to escape into the cold London day. She felt her face remain warm as she offered to take his top hat, gloves and cane leaving him wearing the heavy coat. Possibly he wouldn't notice how chilly the foyer was if he kept it on. He didn't, sweeping the encumbering article from his broad shoulders and laying it across a chair.

The only thing to do was to lead him to the parlor where her knitting was still out and taking up most of the sofa forcing them to stand or sit in the small wingback chairs. She knew she had to begin the conversation and knew it wasn't going to be pleasant.

"I would be the one you need to speak with if it's about Christopher's business." She stood primely, her hands folded in front of her to keep them from shaking with dread. Nothing good could come of this she was sure.

He seemed nonplused as to how to go on now that he knew he had to speak with a woman about whatever had brought him to her home. He must remain standing as long as she stood and she was using that fact to keep this discussion short. He waved her toward one of the chairs and she sighed as she sat knowing he would now be able to become ensconced in a chair himself.

"I should have introduced myself but I didn't realize I was speaking to a family member." She bit her bottom lip knowing that a lady does not open her own front door especially if she has no knowledge of who is behind that door. She said nothing since she had no excuse other than pecuniary reasons which she was not going to discuss with this stranger.

"I am, Lord Leighton." He seemed to expect the name to mean something to her but it did not. She moved nary an eyelash so he continued. "Marquess of Leighton." As if this would explain it better but continued as she did not interrupt him. "Mister Cooper and I have, um, done business together. He was to come to my London address a week ago but failed to show. I was checking to see if, perhaps, he had an accident to prevent him from doing so." He seemed pleased with this announcement although Penny didn't believe it in the least. Not the business part anyways since the man before her did not 'do' business. He had other men do things for him. Perhaps Christopher was owed some money for being one of those that 'did' for Lord Leighton.

"Chr…Mister Cooper is not at home but quite well, I assure you. Perhaps you can relay a message through me and I will pass it on to him when he returns. I'm afraid it will be late so do not expect an answer until tomorrow afternoon."

"Are you by any chance his wife?" His eyes bored into her and she felt uncomfortable answering such a simple question. "N-no, I am his sister, but he tells me everything so whatever brought you to our home can be told to me. I am capable of referring it on to my brother."

Exhaling a long breath, he continued to look at her as if making up his mind about something before speaking. "Are you married?" A rather personal question, but she would think the white mop-cap covering her hair would have indicated her spinster status.

"No, but what difference would it make if I were?" She knew she bristled at the question and was regretting allowing the man to cross her thresh-hold.

He sat back crossing one leg over the other. "A great deal I'm finding out, Miss Cooper."

Her confusion must have shown on her face and he smiled. She thought of a time she watched a cat play with a mouse and for some reason couldn't get the impression she was the mouse out of her mind. "Lord Leighton, perhaps this should wait and you may speak with Christopher when he returns home or I will tell him to attend you at your home tomorrow afternoon." She made as if to rise and he held out his hand to stop her, a silent command which she obeyed.

"Miss Cooper, I expect to see your brother as he promised. I have given him plenty of time to contact Viscount Varley."

Still confused she asked, "Why would he need to contact Viscount Varley, my lord? He hasn't seen him in weeks and then for but a short time at Tattersall's."

He peered at her and she felt like squirming once again but stopped herself from doing such an unladylike movement. "As the viscount's heir, your brother assured me he could get the funds from him. An early installment on his expectation of becoming the viscount, he said."

"Are you sure that is what he said? I mean Viscount Varley doesn't owe Christopher anything." Not actually a lie but not actually revealing the truth either. Closing her eyes, she prayed her brother had a way out of this scrape. Lord Leighton did not appear to be a man who took gambling debt loosely.

His eyes darkened and she felt as if he was holding himself back from saying something. "Can you think of any other form of repayment then? A gentleman's marker needs to be paid upon presenting and now I am expecting some sort of recompense."

Not sure if the man in front of her was actually propositioning her or merely stating things vaguely. Unsure if Christopher had other means of paying besides a draw from future funds as a viscount. She remained calm and silent hoping he would take the hint their conversation was over.

Finally seeming content that she wasn't going to be much help he stood abruptly. "I'll see myself out, if you don't mind. I will accept that you will inform your brother of my visit and my expectations of his future attendance at my home."

Relieved, she stood but made no attempt to follow him. How embarrassing not to be tall enough to help him with his coat or hand his hat back properly. She felt adrift in a new world with this man and she supposed she was. After all, other than the parson and a few of the teachers who also volunteered at the school, no one ever came to her home. She would need to warn Dora if a visit from Lord Leighton was expected or the old woman may have an apoplexy when she saw the Most Honorable Marquess standing on the stoop.

Her knitting sat forgotten on her lap while hours passed waiting for Christopher to return. She hated wasting time but whenever she tried to knit, she couldn't keep her mind on the job and she had had to remove several rows more than once. If she continued, the yarn would be too stretched to knit with properly.

Hearing a key in the door's lock, she pushed the knitting out of the way and rushed to the entrance hoping her brother was sober enough to make sense of the marquess' visit. Her brother entered looking red-eyed and loose mouthed.

Surprised by her presence he cried out, "Penny, you needn't wait up for me. I've been putting myself to bed for years now. No need for a tuck-in." He swayed as he tipped precariously to place his hat on a hook and then stumbled removing his coat.

"Christopher, I need your undivided attention right now. Are you sober enough to think straight?" she asked, hoping this was more of an act to dissuade her from waiting up than an actual state of inebriation.

"Whoa! Way to kill a man's happiness after spending as much as I did on getting in this condition," he admonished her as if she were in the wrong.

Losing what patience she had left after waiting hours for him to come home, she wasn't going to be fobbed off any longer. "Lord Leighton was here today." There let that sink into his rum-sodden brain.

"What? Here, as in this house? Who let him in for

God's sake?" Surprisingly, or perhaps not, Christopher was sounding much soberer as his eyes almost burst from his face.

"I let him in, of course. How was I to know he was here to collect funds owed to him."

"I told you I had gambling debts. Don't act like this is new information, Penny."

So, he was going to place the blame back on her, was he? Because he told her about a gambling debt that covered all sins – like omitting the fact he had been gambling well above his station if he now owed a marquess enough to bring the man to her doorstep looking for payment.

"You intimated that you owed more than you had, but exactly how much do you owe Lord Leighton and are there other markers out there as well? What is the total?"

"Hell, and damnation, Penny, I don't know. It's not like I add them up every day or anything. And my head is pounding so hard I can't think of anything but getting rid of the pain. Is there anything to drink in this place?" He headed toward the dining room.

"No, and I haven't any wine either. Since you rarely eat at home, I have stopped ordering it so you will need to sleep it off, I guess. I don't see us getting to the bottom of this, but you and I will speak about things in the morning. The marquess is expecting you at his door right after noon." She took some joy as he winced at the words and the meaning behind them.

"Aw-w-w, Penny, have a heart. I won't be able to concentrate on anything tomorrow…"

"You can explain that to the Most Honorable Marquess Leighton tomorrow when you see him. I've done my duty to let you know of his arrangements."

"I may have another appointment to see to."

"Do as you will but do not be surprised if the man hunts you down and asks for his money outright in front of your friends and colleagues. He wasn't pleased to be lied to."

"I didn't lie. I merely forgot the time and place we were to meet up."

"He thinks you are Viscount Varley's heir. I don't think he read that in Debretts and then became confused. At least nine people, some of them mere children, would need to perish before your name floated to the top of the list. She left her brother holding his head but thought it best to cut their discussion short and go to her bed before things got out of hand.

CHAPTER THREE

Penny hoped Lord Leighton could wait till the end of the year when their quarterly funds would be available again. Christopher had already worked his way through the third quarter halfway through the summer. She was always playing catch-up trying to stretch the funds to cover past expenses as well as present ones without any chance of saving for the future.

She had hoped to have enough funds to buy a gemmed stickpin for Christopher from the pawn shop, but now it seemed she would be trying to find a way to pawn something instead. Biting her bottom lip, she knew the only thing of value was the small locket she had with the portraits of her mother and father inside. She could keep the miniatures, of course, and that was the locket's real value to her.

There were the books, also, and she had read them all multiple times. That was one thing about her father, he had always known the right book for each person. The book that would mean the most to that individual and become a lifelong favorite.

Even contemplating selling the gifts her parents left her made an ache in her heart, but if it would get Christopher off the hook it would be worth the sacrifice. After all, she was used to sacrifice and she would always have the memories of her parents with or without the books.

Penny hurried across town to reach the school before the children froze waiting for her in the cold rain. The key to the schoolroom was in her reticule tied to the inside of her coat. To carry one over one's arm was tantamount to asking to be robbed or worse on the streets where she was going. Wearing her oldest cloak and plain dress, she usually made it without incident in and out of the slum area where the children needed her most and her brother wanted to help least.

She moved to the far side of the walkway hoping the wheels of the carriage she heard coming up behind her wouldn't splash any higher than her knees. The heat in the schoolroom was nil and she hated to stand in front of the children wet and shivering. It made concentration difficult. Instead of passing, the carriage slowed and a familiar male face appeared in the open window.

"Miss Cooper, how precipitous our meeting like this." The deep male voice called out to her causing others on the street to look her way.

She paused to drop a curtsy, saying, "My lord, I hope you will not think it rude, but I must make a set appointment and am already fearful of being late." She lowered her head so that her face was covered by the poke bonnet and sped-up hoping he would take the hint and be on his way.

"A gentleman cannot leave a lady walking while he rides. My mother taught me better manners than that. Please join me and allow my driver to take you to your appointment."

Without stopping, she said loud enough to be heard over the drip-drops from the buildings' roofs next to her, the whir of the wheels, and clip-clop of horses' hooves, "Thank you but I am almost there, my lord. You best get your head inside or you will be well drenched."

"Then we will be a pair. I'm not sure but I don't think you can get wetter although you can get colder.

Allow me the privilege of delivering you to your destination."

Although she was tempted, the marquess had no idea where she was going and how well his carriage with the crest on the side would be received – by beggars, thieves and cutthroats.

"I am used to the trip for I make it almost daily. Please do not delay your own travels on my account." She looked up and saw several people noting their conversation. It probably looked as if he were trying to pick her up like one of the Winchester Geese. All it needed was a cluster of grapes held out in his hand to complete the scenario.

"My lord, you must desist in this attempt to help me. I am an unmarried woman and you are in an enclosed carriage. The two cannot mix."

"They will mix today or I will follow you to where ever it is that you are going and make sure they realize the danger of fever and fugue they place you in."

She stopped and the carriage did as well. How did he manage that from inside the conveyance as it appeared as if the driver were not paying any attention to her or their conversation? "Oh, I may as well be hanged for a sheep as a lamb, my lord. Please sit back out of the way or I will end up dripping all over you as well as your fine squabs."

He was sitting as far into the corner as he could while chuckling. "An interesting homily I must admit. I knew there was more to you than the mild-mannered young woman who wished me to hades a few days ago."

Startled into explaining, she said, "I did no such thing, my lord. I was simply confused. I hope you and Christopher were able to work out a plan to both your satisfactions." She made sure none of her person touched anywhere near his and that the squish she heard coming from her shoes would soon pass as the water oozed out all over his once clean carpet.

He narrowed his eyes but continued to watch her. The feeling of being a mouse in a cat's gaze was strong but not strong enough to be set down. That reminder of her destination made her watch out the window to see the carriage was going in the correct direction, leaving Cheapside behind. The rain was letting up as well and now she truly resented being forced to accept this man's help.

No words passed between them now that he had his way but she wanted to let him know she did not appreciate being bullied into doing anything she didn't wish to do. "My lord, I must tell you I resent being accosted on my journey and treated like some common street walker." There she said it and her face was hot simply contemplating what he would think of her.

"Hm-m-m-m, a provocative thought but you are hardly a common anything. Right now, you're more of a drowned kitten spitting, hissing, and scratching the hand that is trying to help you."

Admonished, she lowered her head before raising it again saying pleasantly, "I stand corrected, my lord. I should look upon our meeting serendipitously and thank you for your gracious aid." His wide smile was reward enough but as she realized they were already deep into Whitechapel, the carriage came to a standstill in front of the school fronted by small, wet bundles huddled against the building trying to keep dry.

Preparing to dismount without aid, she turned to him. He hadn't moved from his corner. "Thank you, my lord. It was ungracious of me to bring up any of that other."

He smiled again and made a little motion with his hand for her to be off. "Go and teach the little gutter snipes, Miss Cooper. They are in need of your finer feelings more than I."

She was inside trying to coax heat from a central stove by the time she realized the dratted man knew where she was heading and why. How and when did such information come to his notice? Would Christopher have reason to bring up her activities? Possibly blaming her volunteer work as reason for his inability to pay the gambling debt still owed to the marquess?

Pushing all thoughts out of her mind, she concentrated on teaching and getting the children warm and dry before having to send them back out. Some of them lived in a nearby orphanage that rented them out to local manufactories and allowed them to attend school when there wasn't any work. Some lived with their parents who were too poor to care for them during the day and found the school and the free meal fed to the children helped keep the family together. Others, she knew from experience, hid in dark corners and sifted through the refuse of the day for anything edible or saleable. She wished Christopher would visit the school so he could understand how desperately these children needed help.

The day went quickly, the children dreading returning to the cold and wet. Penny sympathized even more as she dragged her feet closing-up and locking the door but if she remained any longer, she would find herself walking in the dark. If Christopher ever found out, he would demand she quit volunteering immediately. This was her only long day as the volunteers referred to it. The day she opened and closed while other days she worked one on one with children helping them learn to read or write. Mathematics was done in a group as was religious training. Several churches helped support the school with funds so it was a mandatory lesson.

Stepping toward the street, her head down, she was startled when she saw a dark shadow lever itself from under the overhang of the building next door and come toward her.

"Miss Cooper, since it did not stop raining, I found myself free to return to escort you home. I hope we will not need to argue about the right or wrong of you riding in an enclosed carriage again."

"No, my lord, I will bow to your superior reasoning. Why should a spinster worry about her reputation over such a thing? I will never face a husband and need to explain about London weather and the feel of soggy shoes on still cold, wet feet."

He held her hand to help her step into his carriage before following her in and sitting into the corner she was beginning to think of as 'his'.

"Tell me about your day, Miss Cooper."

The question surprised her but she thought about it for a moment before saying, "I wished we could afford to feed the children in the mornings when they arrive. They were so cold and wet it took a while to bring their attention to the subject at hand. After the noon meal they were much more settled. Of course, the room had warmed a little too what with cooking the food and heating water. I found boiling water helps heat the room better than only the stove's heat."

"So, you now boil water?"

"I do. I must get water from the pump next door but it is worth the extra work when all is said and done."

"Tell me more." It was dark and difficult to see his expression. She almost asked if he would light one of the interior lamps but then realized he would be able to see her better as well. She knew what she must look like and even if she weren't anything to this man, she was a woman after all and liked to feel attractive. Being a spinster told her she wasn't, but she liked the illusion of thinking so.

"Once the stove was finally burning, we huddled around it and did sums using stories to keep their interest and make it more relevant to them."

"Stories? Like three little pigs?" She heard the laughter behind the words.

"No, my lord, I mean things like farmer Brown had a flock of sheep with one ram and sixteen ewes which would each bear two lambs. In the spring, what did the farmer have?"

Chuckles emitted from the corner. "One very happy ram."

Her face burned with embarrassment. "My lord, that was not well done of you. The children came up with the correct answer and in doing so learned how to add more than two numbers together and double digits as well."

"I commend your loyalty and steadfastness to your students. Not many would be so constant with their time and talent."

"My lord, how do you know so much about me and what I do? Does this have something to do with Christopher needing time to pay you? Do you think I should ask for payment for my time teaching, as he does?"

"Is that what your brother thinks you should do? Take up a position as governess or possibly companion to lessen his cost of you living with him?"

"The annuity is to keep both of us living the lifestyle our father thought we should have and it would if…never mind. It is difficult for a young man on the town to live within limited funds. I understand, I really do."

"You understand he wishes to spend more than the both of you are supposed to live on and then asks for more as if it is an unending pool?" He seemed angry when he had no reason to be. He would get his winnings even if she had to hand-over the next two full quarters of annuity interest to him.

"My brother and I have a very close relationship. Our mother wasn't strong and I took on the responsibility of raising Christopher since he was young. He does not think of me as a sister to protect but as a mother. I have accepted it was partly my fault for his thinking and our father placed the annuity in both our names knowing I would never allow Christopher to go without what he needed."

"And your father has been gone now for how long? Two years?"

She nodded wondering how deeply this man had investigated their heritage. Had he discovered the fact Christopher was not Viscount Varley's heir? Would he discover the truth if he were allowed to keep digging? Realizing the marquess couldn't see her nod, she added, "Yes, in the early spring just as our mother had. It is the worse time for disease to run rife in the slums as people are worn down from the cold and wet and forced to live in confined places."

"We are home, it seems." He began to stir himself and move from his lounging position.

She looked out the window and saw two bright torchieres fronting a huge many-storied house. "Where are we? Christopher will be worried if I'm not home."

"Your brother went out earlier this evening and I know he does not plan on returning until early morning. Please accept my hospitality of dinner and then I'll send you home with a maid as chaperone. This way no one will know you have been in my presence at all."

"No, I must insist I be taken home." She peered into the darkness trying to find something that would tell her where they were and possibly how far she had to walk to her Cheapside address.

"Miss Cooper, do you distrust me?"

"Um, no, it is not that but society has certain beliefs and I volunteer at a facility which depends on church funds and society's benevolence."

She heard him scoff behind her. "Don't lie to me. You are frightened and I have done nothing to provoke such fear. I assure you I only wish to extend our conversation longer. Even you must agree you haven't shared much information with me."

"I did not realize it was a requirement before I reached my home. I would have walked alone in the dark before allowing myself to be put in such a position."

"Such a position? And what position is that, Miss Cooper, I wonder. I only wish to have a nice dinner, a good glass of wine and to learn more about you. I find you fascinating. And, of course, my Aunt Elizabeth would be chaperone enough."

The footman was standing just outside the door and knew he could hear their conversation. Confusion as to why the marquess was doing this kept her mind from thinking of that instead of helping make a decision. "I suppose staying for dinner would be allowed, but only if we are never alone before or after."

His voice sounded relieved. "Agreed, then. Shall we descend and enter my home? I assure you it will be much warmer than this carriage."

The door opened as the footman raised his hand to help her down the steps and onto the carpet leading to the wide door of the house. The smell of the burning oil in the torchiers and the scent of smoke from the many fireplaces tickled her nose. At this point, she eagerly looked forward to the promised warmth behind that shiny black door.

Once inside, a butler stepped up to help her out of her cloak. He didn't say anything, but she knew it was still damp as she watched him motion to a footman to have it brushed out and dried in the laundry room. It had been years since she had been looked after by such a bevy of servants. Her father hired as many of the graduates of the school as he could afford and then after getting experience, they were moved on to other aristocratic homes giving room for new graduates to train.

The marquis motioned towards the stairs. "Mary, please take Miss Cooper upstairs to freshen up. Perhaps you could find her a warm shawl to wear until she dries-out more. It has been a terribly wet day." A young maid curtsied and then took the lead to the next floor up. Penny was left in the room with a fully furnished dressing table, a clean comb and brush at her disposal. She moaned as she dragged the wet hat off her head and saw the tangled mess hiding beneath it.

"Do you need me to help with your hair, Miss? I'm a pretty dab hand at fixing my sisters' hair and hers is naturally curly just like yours. These damp days make it worse."

Penny laughed as she held up hands in defeat seeing the brown mass. "It has been a losing battle for years. I think it's one reason I began wearing the spinster's cap when I was only twenty. I was done trying to fit into society's requirement and it was easier and less expensive. Besides, I have better things to do then to get people to understand my choices."

Mary took first the brush and untangled the long tresses before dividing the hair into portions which she looped and roped and braided quickly forming it all into a neat style that needed few pins to keep it in place.

"Mary, you are a magician." Penny looked from one side to the other turning her head to see all sides in the mirror. Then Mary handed her a soft wool shawl before setting a pair of women's house slippers down for Penny to slip on.

"The marques said that he thought your feet would be warmer in these and I will dry your shoes in the kitchen. There is always heat there."

Penny followed Mary down to a smaller dining room where several footmen waited to service the two people now standing alone there. Penny didn't want to know why the marquess had female clothing in his possession, but felt more at ease having the use of them.

"Thank you, I feel much warmer and more comfortable, my lord."

"Then allow me the privilege of doing more. I have a very good sherry that will help warm you and aid as an aperitif." He handed her a small glass of deep amber liquid and silently toasted her before taking a drink to assure her he dared drink it.

"From the wonderful smells escaping the butler's pantry, I don't think I need any help to my appetite. Morning was a long time ago."

His brows raised in question. "You don't eat with the children. Is the food that bad?"

"The food is relatively good but there is never enough. We get new children every day, especially this time of year. Some come merely to get warm and fed."

"They'd be wiser to learn the lessons you are teaching. It will be an investment in their future." He led her to a chair and helped her sit and took the chair at the head of the table to her left.

"Most of these children don't think they'll have a future so they grab whatever they can at the moment. No one plans for tomorrow because they have seen so many others not make today."

He motioned the footmen to begin the meal service. "Perhaps we should return to you telling me about your life. I know your father was very involved in educating the lower classes but he didn't make his money doing that."

The footman, wearing clean, white cotton gloves, placed a shallow porcelain bowl in front of her as a second did the same to Lord Leighton.

"No, my lord, both Mother and Father were involved in education. Father was a philosophy professor for years and wrote several books which are now used in classes in both Cambridge and Oxford. He put much of those funds in an annuity for his later years. He was about to retire and spend his time teaching and adding new schools in more slum areas within the city."

"And we are right back to your school and the children denied proper care and education." He sipped soup from his spoon. "I can see why your brother might think this school has taken enough of your lives."

She let her hand drop before taking another spoonful. "You agree with him then? That I am wasting my time, my life by trying to help those less fortunate? It would have been me and my brother in that position if our father died earlier than he had, before he could set up the annuity fund. How can you men not recognize that having an educated populace is better for all of us? If everyone could read and write, do sums or have knowledge of a trade there would no longer be an area like the East End where several families are crammed into small rooms without the barest of amenities."

"You are of a mind it is political as well as social? That even if we keep the class division we have now, people could improve their lot?"

She hoped she was hearing what she thought she was hearing from him. "The upper classes should not fear that the lower classes' improvement takes anything away from them. I don't believe taking the money from the rich and giving it to the poor makes everything all right. If I eat well it shouldn't mean that you go without. It means we are all better off...."

"So, you do not expound on the socialistic view of economy? Take from the rich and give to the poor?"

"Isn't that what I just said, my lord? Educating the general populace will do no harm to anyone, but benefit those who receive the education and those who hire them afterwards."

The soup bowls were removed and a baked fish was brought out topped with slices of lemon and sprigs of dill. "This smells wonderful, my lord. My compliments to your chef and I have only had two courses, so far."

"I see we are going to talk of food or get back into the quagmire of educating the lower classes or secure the upper classes' superiority. Possibly the rich worry that if the populace is educated, they will realize the rest of us are not adding anything to the country in any manner."

She snapped her head up and laughed. "That sounds like heresy, my lord. Certainly, you do not say such things in the House of Lords?"

"I do not attend the House so I do not need to hide from anyone when I run into them at a ball or musical. I find I like myself more when I do not get too heated over minor things. Instead, I comfort myself with meeting new people and getting to know them better."

She picked up her refilled glass of very good wine and lifted it as if a toast to him. "I thought we have already decided my life always led back to the same thing – helping the less fortunate through education. It is better if we make this our last visit with one another, my lord. We move in different worlds with different goals. I think it best we have that understanding between us. Christopher will pay you what he owes and then he has promised me he will never play so deep again. It was a young man's folly."

"As you said once before. You and your brother have an unusual relationship and one I think he takes the advantage of."

She finished the chicken breast smothered in a cream sauce with asparagus then patted her lips. "You say that as if you know something I do not. Has Christopher been gambling again? I know it is difficult for a man his age to stay away from the card tables at a ball, but he explained the stakes there are usually low."

He held his glass so that the light flowed through it leaving a rainbow on the white tablecloth. "As you say, it is difficult for some young men to leave the tables when they should."

A dessert tray was brought in and she selected an intriguing chocolate confection along with a filled truffle Lord Leighton forced upon her. She finished with her eyes closed as the rich chocolate flavor with a touch of raspberry melted on her tongue. Opening her eyes, she faced his gaze and unreadable expression.

"My lord, I worried about what tonight would be but this dessert was worth the uncertainty. My appreciation for a very fine meal."

"And as I promised, I will send you home with a companion. Mary will attend you so there will be no talk of my accompanying you alone at night."

Looking at him, she had to ask, "Is there actually an Aunt Elizabeth or did you merely say that to coax me into your home?"

"Do you think I'm the kind of man to say anything untrue to lure a young woman to my dinner table?" His expression did not give the truth away so she had to be content to think there was an Aunt Elizabeth somewhere in his family tree if not this house.

She stood and motioned for him to stay and enjoy his brandy but he shook his head and stood with her. "I will at least walk you to my door and say a proper goodbye." Half way down the passageway to the foyer he stopped and pulled her to him. Bending, he placed his lips softly on hers and pressed. As a kiss it was tame - as a kiss from a handsome marquess it couldn't have been better.

Daniel sat watching the fire, in his sleeping chamber, die into embers. The house had been quiet for hours yet he found he couldn't settle, couldn't stop thinking about Miss Cooper. He supposed he should stop bothering to call her Miss Cooper, at least to himself, since he kissed her. That was the brunt of the problem – why had he kissed her?

He had been with more beautiful women, certainly ones more glamourous and better dressed with some semblance of style. Penelope was one of a kind and perhaps that was what attracted him to her. For he was attracted, had been as soon as he faced her at the door of her home. Not that she tried to entice him, not even after knowing who he was and that her brother owed him money.

But surly beauty was in the eye of the beholder and he could see through her usually plain hairstyle, the unflattering clothes and that mop-cap. She had to have dug that out of a spinster aunt's bottom drawer. None of them hid the natural beauty of her clear complexion, bright hazel eyes that reflected her moods so well, or the golden-brown hair even if she did usually keep it in a tight bun at the nape of her neck. He could see through all of it just as he could see through the artifice of women trying to appear beautiful when they weren't.

No, Miss Cooper was going to be a challenge – to keep his hands off of. Even if he were intrigued, the fact her brother owed him money wasn't going to bring him to the point he would trade anything the woman had for the markers. The markers were his hold over the young man and it would take more than a friendly sister to have Daniel forget the debt and all that it entailed. Instead, he would keep close to the family to find out anything more he should know and if that meant staying close to the man's sister then so be it.

Of course, learning more about them from the investigator he hired should have cooled his blood considerably. She had been schooled by her parents who then took her to every slum area in London setting up schools or private orphanages. Begging outright for funds to run those schools and to open others, even donating more of their own money than he thought the father should have. And being with Penelope, seeing what she would go through to be there for those children no one else seemed to care about, did something to his heart. He didn't think about the children – he thought about her. He couldn't decide whether she wore drab clothing to fit in with the others in the lower districts or because they were inexpensive and she needed to economize.

After spending some time with her, he decided it was both. She was an odd combination of lady and lass, teacher and student, sister and mother. How did she find any time to be herself? She was familiar with nice things, knew what spoon to use when, appreciated good food and wine, yet he knew when she left, she wouldn't pine for anything he had.

He hoped she would think about that kiss. He hadn't meant for it to happen, hadn't meant to taste her lips and then let her go as promised. She also hadn't acted the outraged maiden or compromised miss. Perhaps there was a way to have his cake and eat it too? If he offered to let Cooper's markers burn-up without being redeemed, would his sister thank him in a proper manner? Or rather in an improper manner?

He adjusted his position and brooded. Certainly, a

woman of her age had carnal knowledge if not outright affairs. His investigator found a history of men living in the Cooper house. Even though her brother was supposed to be in residence as well, the time over-lapped Christopher still being at school. Could those men have been there on Penelope's request? He hated to think of her with another man. Having someone else touch her fair skin, see her hair free across a pillow slip, taste those wine kissed lips.

Standing quickly, he gave his manhood more room while pacing. Tonight, there was no coy remarks or flutter of flirtatious lashes. She was open and friendly once she decided to go with him into his home. Friendly, yes, inquisitive as he was about her but he knew when a woman was interested in him and this time, this woman, he couldn't tell completely. Therefore, the kiss. He now knew she was intrigued, but not shocked or dismayed. Not quite the reaction of a woman who had never been kissed – but did she have more experience than that? Could he expect a virgin to pay for her brother's debts with her virtue? Had he slid so far that he would expect it?

He walked back to the table and finished the last of his port before removing his robe and trying to go to sleep.

CHAPTER FOUR

The upcoming Christmas had never seemed so bleak. Penny had to forget her originally planned present for Christopher, but didn't wish him to forego all of the holiday treats. As she walked through the dusting of snow towards the flower vendors, she worried over how that could be accomplished. Today she was planning on buying a few pennies worth of holly for the fireplace mantle. She had red ribbon from past years to place amongst the green and perhaps decorating a Christmas candle to light in the evening would seem celebration enough.

Dora was making a small Christmas pudding and had gathered black walnuts last fall which would be sugared for a special treat as well. With the fine wool yarn Penny had left-over from a shawl she made years ago; Christopher would gain a new neck scarf for under his great-coat. Anything else would need to wait till they were out from under the gambling debts.

Entering the four corners that usually over-flowed with flower vendors, she saw the few still trying to make a sale of winter greens. She was drawn to a small girl, her hair plastered to her head by the melting snow, her nose red from the chilled winds. There was a sad looking pile of holly at her side which appeared to be pieces collected from where the carts had been unloaded.

"Would you care to buy some holly, mum? It looks right festive atop a mantle or such."

Bending down to be more on a plane with the girl, Penny nodded. 'Yes, it is exactly what I had in mind. I'll take all you have." Penny held out more than she was going to pay for Christmas greenery, but knew this was all the girl would see for a day or two.

The girl took her red, raw looking hands from beneath the tatters of a blanket used like a shawl and gathered up the sharp leaves without hesitation or regard for the pain. She put them into the basket Penny held out.

Setting the basket on the ground, Penny unwrapped the scarf from around her neck and placed it on the child's head and over her ears to tie under the small quivering chin. As she removed her own knit gloves, she held them out for the girl's smaller hands. "This is such lovely holly I think I shall leave these with you as well."

"Don't have no money but whut you give me, mum. Here. Takes it back." The child began to unwrap the scarf holding tightly to the pennies.

"No, my dear, the scarf and gloves are a Christmas present for you. I will knit another set so don't think more of it." The young girl stroked the scarf before putting on the gloves. Penny hoped she would keep them and not sell them as soon as Penny was out of sight. Not that she begrudged the little seller a profit, but the girl probably lived out of doors and the added warmth could mean the difference between life and death.

Turning to hurry away now her shopping was complete, hoping the girl had a place safe to go to hide her money, she smacked into a broad cloth-covered wall. A human wall. As she gazed up, she saw Lord Leighton looking down at her with an odd expression. She stepped back awkwardly. "Oh, my lord, I had no idea you were behind me. My apologies for stepping on your boots."

His smile appeared. "There is no problem, Miss Cooper, and you certainly missed my boots." Looking at her hands he asked, "May I carry your basket for you? Do you have other shopping I can escort you to?"

Flustered, she answered more than she wished, "No, I could only afford a small amount of greenery this year and even that came dear. I simply didn't want to let the season pass without any acknowledgment."

"Hm-m-m-m, you there!" He called to a lad the girl was talking with now. "Take three of those bundles of evergreens to that carriage over there and the tiger will pay you."

The boy doffed his hat and ran to pick up the bound boughs.

"It was nice meeting up with you, my lord. Good-bye." She meant to circle round him, but he stepped in front of her before she could and she gazed into his gray eyes, gray as the December sky.

"I came over when I saw you to offer you a ride home. As you see, I took my open carriage out today, endangering my health breathing in all this cold air, simply on the happenstance I would run into you. And *voila* here you are so I think the gods are looking favorably on me. Could I please accompany you home? If not in my carriage then by your side. I'll even stop and buy you chestnuts from the nearest vendor."

She couldn't help but smile. He was being so solicitous and she didn't want to worry over the reason why. Glancing at his carriage and horses which seemed restless standing in the cold and then down the street which was now showing deeper snow then when she came over it made her decision easy. "All right, but we cannot keep making a habit of this, my lord. I have very inquisitive neighbors."

"We all have nosey neighbors but we live with it. I

certainly don't allow them to run my life." During that speech he had guided her to the Landau and helped her up onto the seat which had been protected by a carriage rug now being placed over her legs to hold in her own warmth – and his. She could feel the heat emanating from him and for some reason wanted to lean into it, usurping some of his space.

The tiger jumped on behind holding the boughs in place and Lord Leighton snapped the reins and the horses glided off perfectly without a jerk or shake. It wouldn't take long but it was warmer. Penny would be inside the warmth of her home sooner than if she had walked the several blocks in wet shoes. Why was she always looking like a drown rat with this man? And why was she worried how she looked when he was only here to remind Christopher that he had debts to settle – and soon. The end of the year was but ten days away.

Reaching her small townhouse, she moved to disembark as Lord Leighton hurried to her side. "Thank you very much, my lord. I won't keep you since I'm sure the horses would like to get back to a nice, warm stable."

"The horses would like a nice long run but in town it isn't possible." Motioning to the tiger. "Here, Gordon, carry the boughs to the side by the kitchen door and then take the horses for a real run. I'll wait here or walk back after tea." He turned to her standing beside him asking innocently, "You were going to offer me tea, weren't you, for bringing you home?"

"Ah, oh, of course, my lord. Yes, tea…."

She let herself in with the large man behind her wondering how this had happened to her. She was going to be alone with this man again and she had no polite way of turning him out. After all he had done her a favor, she

35

had accepted that favor and by society's rules owed him tea at least.

Taking off her snow-covered bonnet, she shook it out over the rug and then sat it on a marble topped table to dry. He removed his top hat and set it next to hers, then opened his coat placing it across the chair as he did along with his driving gloves. She showed him into the parlor and went in search of Dora. Firstly, because the woman had never been summoned by the bell-pull in the parlor and probably wouldn't know where to go and secondly, to get some time away from the marquess so she could think. His presence sent any brain she thought she had into some kind of dance skittering all over the place, wishing for mad things that could never occur – not between the two of them, at least.

Arriving back to find him fingering the pile of finished scarves, he looked up with a smile. "All set, now? Perhaps you can explain these for me?"

Surprised, she asked, "The scarves and mittens? Why, they are for the children. All accept that one on the end. That longer one is for Christopher for Christmas morning. We have always gotten one another gifts…ever since Father passed. Before that, Father got us something each year.

"Like that pendant around your neck you finger whenever you get nervous?"

She dropped the favored gift like a hot brick. "Yes, like this. Mostly books but I have a cherished library now that I can read and remember exactly when he gave each book to me."

He moved about the room like a slow, menacing panther. Was he trying to size up everything in the room? Calculate what each would bring on the auction block. If he was knowledgeable, he knew it wasn't much. They bought quality when they could. but nothing besides essential items were purchased for the home use. Any extra money would have gone back into the annuity or the slum schools themselves. She notched her chin higher knowing her household goods would come up wanting.

"Did your brother receive the same? I mean did your father treat him any better being as he would one day be a viscount?" He turned his calculating eyes upon her and waited for an answer.

Thankfully Dora came in doing an admirable job of balancing the tea things and Penny rushed to help her set it on the newly cleared table. Dora tried a shaky curtsy. "Will there be anything else, Miss?"

Feeling pride that the older woman would try to act as if this was a daily occurrence, Penny smiled and said, "No, Dora, that should be all."

Penny's heart dropped when she saw the plate piled with the ginger-snaps she had baked for Cristopher's Christmas tea. Hopefully Dora kept a few back but it didn't look like it. Perhaps Lord Leighton didn't like the spicy morsels and would leave after drinking one cup of tea. After all, there really wasn't much here of interest to him.

She poured him a cup of tea, plain as he requested, and handed it to him. Picking up the plate of cookies, his brows rose in interest. He held his cup and saucer out to her as she placed a cookie on the side, then another as he continued to hold it out before accepting the cup to his lips.

"You never answered my question. Did your father treat the two of you differently?"

This question, at least, she could answer without perjuring herself. "Not really although Christopher was sent away to school. Cambridge, since Father hoped his son would become a philosopher as he was or possibly go into the church. Unfortunately, Christopher wasn't interested in either field."

"Why do you do that, I wonder? Why do we always end up speaking of Christopher when I ask about you?" He reached over for another two cookies taking one and snapping it in half between his even, white teeth. She found herself practically mesmerized by his chewing.

"I do not. It's just that a lady doesn't talk about herself."

"If you think that's true then you've never been to a debutant ball. I have and it's all they ever wish to talk about no matter how you try to get them to say something meaningful that wasn't a rude remark about one of the other debutants." He dusted off his fingers and looked longingly at the now half-eaten plate of cookies. She tried not to roll her eyes as she offered the plate to him once more. He quickly took two again with a smile and devoured one with a quick pop into his mouth.

"I answered your question which I must point out seems rather rude to me. My father left me executor of his estate stipulating it would go to Christopher upon my marriage. It isn't exactly as his solicitors advised him, but it is the way it was written since Christopher hadn't reached his majority yet."

"And I agree with his decision. Your brother hasn't the maturity to handle any sizable fund, but he has promise, I think, with you as his guide."

"Thank you, I think, my lord. My father was merely being practical. A schoolboy should not be placed in charge of money nor should he carry the weight of caring for his older sister for the rest of her life."

"The rest of your life?" His brows rose in inquiry. "You never plan to marry then? Never plan to give up the reins to the coffer?"

"No, not the reins part, at least. When I think him ready, I will give up all control of father's annuity but that doesn't seem to be yet."

"If he becomes Viscount Varley will you hand it over then?"

Not exactly telling a lie, she answered, "When Christopher becomes Viscount Varley, I will sign over all rights to his control." Picking up the tea pot she asked, "Would you care for more tea?"

His smile in return was unreadable. "Certainly, and a couple more of those ginger things, too, please." He accepted two more. "I think I am becoming addicted to these little bites of heaven. Perhaps we can make some kind of arrangements for them to be ready for me whenever I wish to stop by? You know, smelling wonderful and tasting like sugar and spice?"

She wished she knew if that was a metaphor for anything or if the man was mad enough to accept gingersnaps in lieu of gambling debts in the dozens of pounds? How did she answer when she wasn't sure what the question was? Did the man enjoy toying with her? Drive her insane waiting for his demand that she pay him in cash or in kind as he threatened when he first came to her home?

Soon there was no more tea and only crumbs left on the cookie plate. "I know I've over stayed my visit. I was so comfortable here by the fire with our stimulating conversation but I see Gordon outside for me. Could you have your cook write down the recipe for the ginger biscuits for me so I can give it to my baker? I have never enjoyed anything more."

Hoping to get rid of him sooner, she offered, "I can give it to you right now, my lord. It is an old family favorite for this time of year." She went to the small writing table in the corner and set to writing down the ingredients from memory since she baked the cookies herself.

Watching him drive off with the sheet of paper tucked into his coat pocket, Penny hoped next time he wouldn't eat all the cookies. Of course, next time would have to be next Christmas since she had used up all of the expensive ginger and sugar this year. She was happy he'd taken his tea plain or there would have been an embarrassing moment and honey would be her only offering. Dora's brother brought in honey from the country every fall so they had plenty of that at the time.

Bursting into the room, Christopher shed his coat letting it drop to the carpet. "Penny, did I just see Lord Leighton driving away from this street? Why was he here?" He looked flushed and red nosed but not from drink. She couldn't smell any alcohol on him so it must be from the cold and worry over the markers.

"Yes, he drove me home – in an open carriage as you see and I offered him tea in recompense. He said nothing about the markers."

Her brother paced the room. "But you spoke of me? My prospects? Did he ask about my becoming viscount?" The questions were shot at her as if from a cannon.

"In a way he did but I neither said you were or were not to be viscount one day. He kept asking about me, about how Father raised us…things like that."

"Oh, God, he isn't going to ever agree." He buried his head in both his hands and slumped onto the sofa.

Penny sat beside him trying to make sense of his words, of why Lord Leighton's interest in them would matter one way or another. She was sure the marquess had been trying to find something of value he could exchange for the gambling debt. "Dearest, what isn't he going to agree to? Did you try to make a deal to pay off the markers over a few months?"

He turned to Penny with tears in his eyes. She had never seen him so distraught. "I haven't told you everything, nothing bad, but you don't know everything."

"I can't help but wonder how you met the man. You certainly don't run in the same circles, do you? He seems so much older."

"It's Julia. Lady Julia, Lord Leighton's sister's oldest daughter. I love her but she's come out this season and everyone's saying she will 'take'. Engaged by the end of the season and it won't be to a penniless son of a philosophy professor."

"Oh, my dearest. I am so sorry it couldn't be different, but why gamble and with her uncle no less? If he knew how you got the money, he certainly wouldn't think you worth his niece." She petted his hair as she used to when he was ill and it always made him feel better. But he wasn't a little boy any longer and this wasn't an upset tummy.

"I should have thought things through more, but he showed up at the Henderson Ball and Julia urged me to at least speak with him, you know, introduce myself so she and I could dance together."

"You hadn't even danced with her but think you should be married? Christopher, are you gone mad?"

"Don't think I and half my friends haven't asked the same thing. Anyway, there was an open chair at his table so I asked to join and they all accepted me. After all, I was a guest just as they were and my money was as good as theirs. It's simply that I don't have the kind of money they were betting. I should have excused myself after the first hand. I'm used to playing for half-pence a point with the boys at school not this cutthroat game they laid out."

"So, you ended up betting more than you had and he accepted your markers. Why not stop then?" She never thought her brother would allow himself to be taken, but it almost sounded as if Lord Leighton and his friends set out to fleece Christopher.

"I tried but Lord Leighton kept saying it was only a friendly game among men and it seemed as if he was accepting me into his group. He called me by my first name and told me to call him Leighton. It seemed too good to be true and then it all happened so fast. It was a big pot and I had the best hand of the night. I bet it all and then, swoosh, Lord Leighton won, stood up and slapped a couple of the other men on their shoulders and they all walked out on me without another word. As if I wasn't there except for the markers which he pocketed before leaving."

"It does sound as if he scammed you. Does he know about you and Lady Julia?" Penny was trying to find some reason a marquess would need to befriend and then indebt a young man not of the peerage. And why keep finding ways to get into the house or question her? What other game was Lord Leighton playing with them?

"Julia says neither her mother or uncle has said

anything to her about me so perhaps it has nothing to do with her and I."

"I find that difficult to believe. But how did you meet Lady Julia in the first place?"

"I went to school with Archibald, who is now a baron and has been ordered to find a bride among this year's debutants. He's the last of the line and his mother insists he wed and get an heir as soon as possible. He didn't want to face what he called the horde of eager mamas and their man-eating daughters alone so took me along to these balls he had invitations to."

"And you met Lady Julia who won your heart?"

"Don't make it sound as if it doesn't count or mean anything, Penny. We met but since her mother did not know me or my family, I wasn't allowed to ask for a dance. Instead, we snuck away for lemonade and talked. We found we liked one another very much and that turned to love so quickly I barely had time to blink."

Trying to dissuade Christopher, she asked, "But perhaps by falling in love so quickly it may be a crush instead? I mean, you are both so young and as you said this is her first season. Many young girls have several seasons before they wed. If her feelings are as strong as yours, she can remain true for another year."

He stood, letting go of her hands and stepping away. "And in a year what will have changed except that I may have paid off some of my markers?"

She felt dread like a cold evil thing crawl up her back and try to suffocate her. "Christopher, how much exactly do you owe, Lord Leighton?"

"Over five-hundred pounds." He collapsed onto the chair as if merely saying the amount deflated him completely.

"Oh-h-h, Christopher, how are we to repay that kind of money? It's more than the annuity pays us in a year. I know there isn't a way to get the solicitors to allow us any more than that. It is based on the interest of the bonds father bought." Tears were in her eyes as she watched her brother sink even lower in the chair. Not only were they not going to be able to pay off the debt at the first of the year, they wouldn't be able to pay off the debt at the end of next year, either. Even if they could keep the interest on the markers low, it would take all they had.

CHAPTER FIVE

Pouring himself an overly liberal portion of brandy from the decanter in his private library, Daniel thought of the conversation he had with Miss Cooper. How did one understand someone so different? Miss Cooper. He found thinking of her more formally kept him from thinking about her more personally. He searched her face, her movements, her every word trying to find the reason for his constant thoughts of her. What she was doing, was she warm, hungry, in need of anything he could offer?

Today he tried to get her to be honest with him about her brother. At least agree the man is not worth her worry or her attentions. He thought Cooper a man who would do anything to make his way in society, a society he did not and would never be a part of. But no matter how he worded the question, Miss Cooper answered without giving away the fact her brother was not to inherit the Varley title. Was not close even if the present viscount were eighty-years-old with one foot in the grave. Which he was not. She allowed the lie her brother told to stay in place although he could see she didn't relish the lie herself. Always turning away whenever the subject was brought up in conversation.

How was he to help if they both refused to be honest with him? He could see that Cooper's feeling for his niece were true even if encouraged by the large dowry Julia would receive upon her marriage but only if Daniel, as her legal guardian, approved of the prospective groom. Christopher Cooper was not that groom. Having a good education and being able to take to the dance floor while pointing a slender foot, making the proper greeting and bow to a titled person did not make him husband material for his niece.

Julia had already made her thoughts and wishes known, throwing a temper-tantrum when his sister told her daughter she could no longer accept Cooper's name on her dance card nor take supper sitting beside him. He might have handled his niece in a different manner but then he had Margaret, Julia's mother, to contend with at her come-out. The two females were very much alike, but he didn't think his sister was up to hearing that at the moment.

The real problem wasn't with Margaret or Julia. Not even with Cooper who he could have driven out of London's society by merely letting it be known he hadn't paid-off his markers yet. No, the problem was with him and his growing desire for Cooper's sister. No matter how often they spoke, he felt driven to search her out. No matter how banal their conversation he felt invigorated and more alive being in the same space as she, breathing the same air.

Desire slammed into his gut as if taking a physical blow. That was the problem. He, Danial Waite, Marquess Leighton, was smitten by a simple woman without any redeeming beauty or wealth. Completely opposite of what he thought he would need and want in a wife or any woman he bedded. Instead, he was trying to find a way of defeating her brother in his attempt to compromise his niece while at the same time trying to bed the man's sister.

Would he allow the man to keep pursuing Julia simply to keep the man's sister within reach? As long as

Cooper thought he had a chance, he will stay in London. Everyone knows it is less expensive to live outside the city, to move to a village cottage where the quarterly payments would go farther. But if Cooper were driven from town then his sister would go with him. Where else could she go?

Daniel wasn't foolish enough to think Penelope would consent to become his mistress. Not if he wasn't going to consent to leaving her brother as he is. Fancy free and trying his best to get a rich bride using a lie of a possible title in his future. The little fool. The proverb penny wise and pound foolish came to mind more often of late. Miss Cooper couldn't see the benefit of being taken care of by him, but would scratch out an extra farthing for coal for that school she supported.

Slamming his now empty glass onto his desk, he wished he had strength enough to simply tell the man to leave or be exposed for the fraud he was. Embarrass him into leaving society if not London completely. Whenever he thought of the aftermath of such a thing, all he could see were the tears in Penelope's eyes, the hurt and pain he had caused her.

Turning away, hoping to leave his contemplations in the library, he left to seek out some semblance of relief from his thoughts. He headed to the little house on Curzon Street he knew always had a welcome for him.

CHAPTER SIX

The rapping of the door announced another visitor. Like the others recently, Penny was sure it would not be Father Christmas or any other light-hearted soul to help them. She was correct when she found Lord Leighton standing there with a tall, fat beeswax candle in a basket. Holding it up, he smiled saying, "In repayment for those gingersnaps. I thought this Christmas candle would look good in the holly on the mantle." He waited while she tried to find a reason not to accept the innocuous gift. After all, this man was hopefully going to give them time to repay the gambling debts and she should keep him up sweet.

"That was very kind of you, my lord." She attempted to take the basket but he held it up higher and stepped in forcing her to back into her own foyer while making room for the large man.

He sat the basket down and began removing his coat and hat, acting so much like a man who belonged in her foyer she was stymied as to how to go on. "I, ah, would you care for tea? I'm afraid I don't have any more gingersnaps, but perhaps some bread and butter would do if you are peckish?"

"Perhaps there will be some by the end of the afternoon. Gordon is dropping off a few things to your maid. I was hoping to get more by then or I can send Gordon back for them. My cook's best efforts weren't as tasty." He turned a suspicious gaze towards her. "Or did you leave something out of the ingredients so I must return to you?"

Indignant, Penny huffed, "I most certainly did not, I assure you. I make them every year and never use a written recipe. There was nothing left out."

"That's what cook assured me, also, saying everything looked correct and they weren't burnt but his simply were not as good."

Trying to remain sounding generous, she said, "I will gladly bake you some and send them over to your home or you may send Gordon back for them. They will take about an hour I would say." She did not budge from the foyer but remained there as if waiting for his compliance.

"Let's see to that tea first. I'm sure I can live for another day without the biscuits. Christmas always brings out the small boy in me and I get greedy, I suppose." He was in the parlor before she could keep him out and followed him, deciding to take charge of this invasion before she threw him out. His autocratic actions were rubbing against the daughter of a philosopher who believed all men were created equal and could raise themselves if they wished or fall to the lowest form of man if they did not heed the rules of life and society.

Standing with his hands clasped behind his back, he looked at the holly dotted with red bows on the mantle humming. Completely at home while she felt as if she were the uninvited interloper. "I'll see to the tea since Dora will be quite busy at this time of day." Even her inference he was there at a bad time didn't get the man to realize he should be leaving.

Stomping to the kitchen, Penny had to listen to Dora go on and on about the 'lovely' supplies his lordship had sent them. Candied fruit for cake, flour, sugar, eggs, and several spices including ginger and nutmeg. Dora was acting as if it were manna from heaven and in a way, it was. It had been years since the larder had held so many rich ingredients at one time.

Penny added a bowl of sugar to the tea tray and carried it back to the parlor herself. Lord Leighton may not take sugar in his tea but Penny was going to get some kind of reward for putting up with the man two days in a row.

"Here we are. I'm afraid I didn't take time to fix the bread and butter knowing you will wish to be on your way, but I'm sure you can get all you want when you reach home. After all, it isn't too far away now, is it?" She poured quickly, spilling tea into the saucer without apology. For some reason she was furious with him for sending the foodstuff, for bringing the candle, for being rich and handsome and for feeling superior to her and her brother.

He stared at her down his aristocratic nose and then had the audacity to ask, "Are you peeved with me, Miss Cooper?"

"Peeved, my lord? I don't think that covers my feelings for you." She dumped two spoonsful of sugar into her tea and stirred furiously.

Smirking, he asked, taking a sip from his cup, "Did the tea do something to you as well? Perhaps we both deserve an explanation."

"I need to explain to you? How do I explain a young man's regard of an older, wiser gentleman who then fleeces that young man of everything he ever wanted or desired? You and your friends knew exactly what you were doing. Egging Christopher on to bet higher and higher stakes knowing he was barely out of school…."

"A Gentleman," he emphasized the second word,

"knows when to toss in his hand. When to bow and leave the game, when he has been outplayed and outwitted by others at the table. I assume your father never taught him that, but surely he picked-up something from other students at Cambridge."

"How smug you sound. How sure of yourself, but you are correct in that Christopher had no males to help him gain town bronze. Merely a few other students on their way to manhood. It wouldn't kill the rest of you to help them along the way." She gulped her hot tea in one swig and ended up coughing and rubbing tears from her eyes which were not all caused by the choking. "He sought you out because he wanted to make your acquaintance, not get a lesson on gambling. He, he wished to socialize, is all."

"You think I should help him worm his way into my niece's life? She is barely out of the schoolroom and yet your brother, without a feather to fly with, living on his sister's endeavors, dares to talk her into 'waiting' for him. Waiting for what? Some middle-aged man to die so he can inherit a viscount title? My sister is devastated her daughter refuses half their invitations since your brother can attend only those of more liberal minded peers."

Penny was distressed knowing others knew about Christopher and Julia after her brother had been so sure no one suspected. She sat unable to do anything but listen to another side of the problem. Lord Leighton evidently knew of Christopher's interest in Julia as he continued. "As the male head of the family, I take my duty to my sister and niece seriously. My sister spent time and money on dresses Julia refuses to wear, places she refuses to go, people she refuses to meet."

Heated, Penny needed to point out Julia's view.

"You mean other young men? Young men with titles already or much sooner to come into them than someone like Christopher? Doesn't the young woman's wishes mean anything?"

"She is too young to make that kind of a decision and if you had ever met her, you would understand. She thinks their relationship is destined, that their 'love' will outlast the difficulties facing them. She has no idea how much pressure will be on her if she marries so far beneath herself."

"Christopher is not of the peerage, may never be more than a professor's son, but my father was a good man, an honorable man, and I will not allow anyone to say otherwise. Get out! Get out of my house!" She pointed toward the foyer, tears blinding her to anything but her anger towards this man who saw everything exactly as what her father fought against. The rich taking more from the world then they needed, selfishly keeping it limited to ten thousand people or so, even looking down on their own for not being of high enough rank to matter.

How could Christopher ever become what he wanted, marry the woman he loved? Penny was certain Christopher had covered all this kind of thinking already, thought he understood what he would need to overcome, but men like this lord would knock him back at each step.

Lord Leighton came up behind her. She sensed him approach, felt his warm breath on the nape of her neck. She trembled but not only in fear. In acknowledgment of his virility and her unsureness of him, the unknown of what to expect.

"You'd do anything to protect your brother, wouldn't you? There would be no limit if you thought you could keep him from debtor's prison, from being named a fraud. These are not questions, but statements and I would like to hear the answer from your lips."

She gazed at the floor, trembling and flushed. What was he up to now? How much more could he humiliate her by repeating how unsophisticated her brother was, her father, her family? He had no right to set the rules, keep people apart, ruin everything beautiful in life.

"Simply nod if I have the truth of it." He continued to confront her, questioning her as if he had the right to speak to her in such a manner.

She wasn't sure what he was hinting at, but if it was to give up her virtue then he was correct – she would even sacrifice her body to keep Christopher safe from any harm. Given a chance to marry the young woman he loved and whose dowry would be her brother's salvation. She thought she'd finally learn her lesson in a very dangerous way. If laying with this man insured Cristopher's happiness then she would face the consequences later. Biting her bottom lip, she nodded and quickly glanced over her shoulder to find he had moved away. Exhaling the breath, she unconsciously held, her body practically slumped in relief of not having him hawking over her.

He was standing nonchalantly next to the tea service pouring another cup of tea and adding sugar. He brought it to her warning, "It's still hot."

She bent her head and mumbled, "What are you suggesting, my lord?"

"Do I need to put it into words, my dear?" At her silence, he continued, "I could be led to forgetting your brother's debt and the fact he compromised my niece by meeting with her surreptitiously at museums and churches for the past few weeks. I would even go as far as to say I will introduce him to the right people and help him find a job such as steward or rector - anything other than Julia's husband. He would need to promise to stay away from my family and let nature take its course as to Julia's future. She has years ahead of her and her dowry alone would attract any number of titled young men."

He reached out and she tried not to flinch at his touch. It was hot instead of the cold reptilian feel she expected. What kind of man gives his own poor view on another man, yet, at the same time, offers to change that view if a woman would sleep with him? How much her father hadn't told her, yet, she now knew to be true about the world. Hypocrisy runs rampant and gentleman and gentlemanly are worlds apart.

"If I give myself to you, then you will tear up the markers? You will not do anything to harm my brother? I cannot promise that he will give up Julia so easily but at least he will go forward without owing you a farthing."

His hands stroked down her arms and ended with his head just above her ear as he whispered, "I can protect Julia and your brother will be as he began. Without an extra pound to his name and his sister paying his debts." Then he kissed her neck and she almost screamed with the sensations welling inside her – and they weren't all repulsive. She moved quickly trying to ease the touch of him from her sensitive skin. She could not allow him to know how he affected her, could not allow him to guess he could have her without any benefit to Christopher.

She was agitated and wasn't thinking straight. What had he meant by touching her like that? Talking to her like that? She didn't understand everything he was saying but she understood his intent. He was half-seducing her and half-telling her what he planned on doing to her – with or without her permission. Christopher's debts would be paid one way or another. How was she to get out of this predicament? If she refused him entrance to her home in the future would he change his mind and call in the notes? Ruin Christopher and send them both to debtor's prison?

Following her, he pressed her up against the parlor's wall and inhaled deeply finding something calming in her scent, being close to her as if he had the right to reach out and twine the escaping curl around his finger as he was doing. Or to tuck it back behind her ear, the skin so soft and inviting he sniffed there as well. Like a sweet fruit or flower, yet, he didn't think she wore a perfume, merely her own sweet fragrance. "I ache for you and you stand there as if butter wouldn't melt in your mouth – so cool and in control of your emotions while I…I just want to bury myself in you."

He covered her lips and kissed her deeply, savoring her inner mouth with a stroke of his tongue. Feeling her knees give way, he clasped her closer to his chest wishing they were somewhere more private now that she had decided she may as well pay the debt owed. He no longer cared whether she was worth the amount of the markers or not. To him she would be, even if she were the most untried harlot. She would be worth them to be free of this burning desire for her and to crush her virtuous spinster act.

"If I slipped my hand under your skirts would you be wet for me? Offer me more than merely a touch of your satiny channel? Give me solace with your warmth and nestle me between your silken thighs?"

Why was he torturing himself in this manner? Why

wasn't he picking her up and rushing her upstairs to take what he had been offered in compensation for what he was owed. Once that was done, he could cut all ties with the Cooper family and the way this woman made him feel. He found getting into the gutters wasn't as easy as he thought. The draw was immense but getting one to feel clean again was going to take longer than he imagined.

Penelope was so much more than he thought she would be, meant so much more than he thought she could. All to catch a man who had set his eye on his niece and her dowry. Christopher didn't deserve the loyalty from either of the women concerned and it was up to him to show Julia the true nature of her brother. That Cooper would allow his own sister to sell what virtue she had to keep from paying his gambling debts was like an aphrodisiac. Never had Daniel wanted a woman more. But what happens the next time? If Daniel didn't put an end to things between the fraud and his niece, would Christopher offer up his wife, as well, when next the man found himself short of funds?

The sister was too loyal. Too honest for her own good. Too willing to martyr herself for a brother Daniel doubted would appreciate her sacrifice.

He pushed her away, allowing her to return to the sofa. Far enough away for him to regain his senses – his moral balance.

CHAPTER SEVEN

"Why are there no candles lit, Penny?" Christopher burst into the room, pushing open the almost closed door to the foyer and lighting a candle before looking around to see her sitting with Lord Leighton standing beside her. His eyes narrowed as he took in the two people.

"Leighton, what's going on here? Did you come to speak with me about the markers? I told you I would meet with you at your house if we must go over things again."

"I found your sister much easier to make arrangements with. I told you I'm not a man with patience." She knew the man's gaze remained on her brother as the marquess ignored her at his side.

"Penny, what is he talking about? I told you he was dangerous and to keep your distance. Now, I find you having tea alone in a darkened room." He seemed older somehow and she knew this could end badly if she couldn't dislodge the burning fuse.

"We were so engrossed in our conversation I'm afraid it became dark without either of us realizing. It must have just occurred. There is nothing more to it than that." She smiled although Christopher was staring at Lord Leighton and not even looking her direction.

"Cooper, I think you best allow the grown-ups to reach a grown-up solution to your problems. Penelope and I are in agreement as to how to proceed." The marquess' words cut through air between them.

"Do not dare use my sister's Christian name. You have not made any agreement and I will not allow her to speak for me. What kind of a brother do you think me? What kind of man to allow you to stand in my home and insinuate my sister is some kind of chattel I've given you use of?"

"Now, son, you must realize you owe me more than you can ever repay." It was almost as if Lord Leighton was choosing every word, he could, to inflame Christopher.

"If I do, it is my own fault and I will pay the consequences. If I end up in debtor's prison then so be it. If it costs me the woman I love, she knows I have tried my best for us. But I will not allow you to besmirch my sister's character in such a way. I will see you on the field of honor in the morning."

She jumped up and raced to her brother's side trying to get him to look into her eyes, hear her words. "Christopher, do not say such a thing. We were simply talking. He hasn't laid a hand on me. I haven't agreed to anything. He isn't worth it. Father would agree with me and you know it. His kind aren't worth a tenth of yours."

She saw Lord Leighton walk toward the lighted foyer. "You would face me and one of my many dueling pistols in the morning to keep me from paying-off your markers by using your sister? Knowing that in doing so, you would never be allowed to see Julia again?"

"It doesn't mean I love Julia any less, but I will not allow you to be near Penny again. I will protect her with my life and if I fail, it is all I can give."

His lordship's expression was unreadable. "Then I will see you in the park at six of the clock tomorrow. Bring a witness."

"I have friends who will act as my second, Leighton. Do not worry you will have a body to contend with at the end of things. After what I think has been going on in here, you are not a gentleman and should not be left to live as one."

"I also have friends who will act as my second. But you needn't bring a doctor because I plan on hitting my mark."

Lord Leighton left as Penny hugged her brother. "Oh, Christopher, what have you done? We can wait a while and send a note retracting your ultimatum. It is only the three of us who know of your challenge."

"Yes, and I am a gentleman and Leighton has proven himself not to be. I knew he was up to something when Julia disappeared from society and he was with you too often. A man like him only 'slums it' when he's up to no good. I'm sorry my actions brought him to our door, to you."

"I could have sent him away only I thought, if we remained on good terms, he would allow you to see Julia. That is if he even knew of it and, also, to give us more time to pay off the markers."

"Promise me if he tries to collect that you won't pay it. I'm not certain any longer it was a fair game. I've asked around and no one had ever heard of Leighton and his friends playing so deeply at a private ball. It was almost as if I were set-up to end owing him."

"Don't speak as if you don't plan on coming back to me. You're the only thing I live for, the only reason for me to go on." She clutched at him but she knew he was leaving her. She was losing him already. "Cristopher, listen to me. There may be another way to get out of all this. We need to stop this from going any further." She was placing her hands on him. On his hands, his arms, his shoulders trying to keep him close while convincing him not to go to the park in the morning. His life would be lost for nothing, and all over a proposition she never planned on accepting. No matter how much she relished the idea of Leighton's touch.

She cried for a few minutes after Christopher left, explaining his need to get a second, before grabbing her cape and hat. Getting Lord Leighton to decline the challenge, to arrange some kind of payment plan they could meet was priority. As for Julia, the girl would need to do as her parent wanted her to do until she married or gained her majority. Hopefully, Cristopher would outgrow his puppy-love without going through too much pain.

She bundled the cloak closer to her neck, not having taken time to get ready for the long walk in the cold December night. The gas lights were dim through the flurries of snow as she moved slowly checking what street signs she could find as the snow increased and built up on surfaces. A few carriages were out, but the horses wore blankets and the drivers muffled up to their noses, both ignoring the shivering woman making her way to St. James Street.

Penny lifted the knocker and let it drop on the shiny black door. The torchiers were unlit this night since the household evidently was staying in. Her hands seemed numb, but she hadn't replaced the gloves she gave away, yet, and didn't think to find any others. If she had stayed and thought too much about what she planned to do, she wouldn't have enough courage to go forward. A butler opened the door, looking over her head peering into the darkness.

She called out, getting his attention over the sounds of the wind swirling the snow around them, "My name is Penelope Cooper and I wish to speak to Lord Leighton. It is a matter of life and death – his." There, see if the man was brave enough to ignore that provocative statement.

"Please wait here, madam." Then the door was shut and all light disappeared as she stood in the cold, dark night.

The door opened almost immediately and Lord Leighton stepped out lifting her into the house and setting her down chaffing her hands between his larger ones. "Penelope, is it now?" He looked over to Mary who arrived with a shawl and slippers. "Here take off those wet shoes. Mary, is there a fire in the blue room or the library?"

"The library is warm, my lord, and one is laid but unlit in the blue room," answered the familiar maid.

Penny pushed away from him and tried to straighten her plain skirt looking anywhere but at the butler or footmen lining the wall. Mary placed the shawl over her shoulders and slipped on the warm footwear so there was immediate relief to her cold toes.

She turned to Lord Leighton. "We need to talk – I couldn't keep Christopher from finding a second." Now she was wringing her own hands due to worry.

A squeak came from the entrance to the rest of the house. "Christopher? You're talking about Christopher?" A lovely blond-haired girl rushed into the now crowded foyer with a lovely older lady who looked much like the younger version. "You must be Penny, I so wanted to meet you before…before I left for the country." The young woman said eager to speak before someone pulled her away.

Penny didn't want to say too much, hoping to keep

the duel as quiet as possible so that if she could convince at least one of the combatants to refuse to show, then no one would end up wounded or dead. Either event is against the law and the one left alive would be arrested and hung or would need to leave the country.

"Yes, you must be, Lady Julia. He has spoken highly of you. It is good to meet you, but I must excuse my manner of dress. I wasn't planning on meeting anyone as I had some business with Lord Leighton. He, um, he is one of the benefactors of a school I support."

"Julia, we mustn't keep Miss Cooper and your uncle from their talk. I'm sure he'll be in by the time dinner is called." A warning or an order? Penny wasn't certain but Lady Julia's mother didn't seem like the kind who needed any man's help with anything.

Lord Leighton's hand was on her arm and steering her down lighted halls past open doors showing well furnished rooms, many with fires already present. Still they walked on until he moved her into a library with floor to ceiling filled bookshelves. Penny didn't bother reading the titles. They meant nothing to her and she had too important an errand to waste time on trivial things.

As they came to a stop, she turned on her host. "I am begging you to call off this duel. I will do anything, you understand? Anything to save my brother from this disastrous declaration. I know he did not follow society's dictates, but that is no reason for him to pay with his life."

"No, but you would pay with yours? You know what society will say and do to a woman who has fallen so far?" His gray eyes seemed to glimmer in the light thrown from the fireplace.

"It doesn't matter. I work with women like that

every day. Women who had no other way to feed or protect their family. I will be no better or worse than they."

He shrugged and stepped away from her. "You needn't worry for your virtue although I cannot say I wasn't tempted. Mostly I wanted to see if Christopher would show his true self. Your brother has made many promises he couldn't live up to. I wondered if the ruse he wished to talk was to be simply one more. He surprised me, he does have scruples and wasn't using you in payment of the debts. I apologize for my ill treatment of you and for any discomfort I may have caused you."

"So, you will allow Christopher to repay the markers without causing him any problems? I will try to remind him about staying away from Julia, but with what she said in the foyer, it sounds as if she is leaving."

"That was one of the possibilities. Since she doesn't want a season with the restrictions her mother feels are for Julia's own safety, they have been talking of returning to the country. Try again in the coming year."

"Then there won't be any chance of them meeting again." She knew her brother would be heartbroken. "It will not be easy for Christopher, but he will manage. You already know my view."

"I do."

She moved to pass him and leave, happy to be done with him but sad for the outcome. "I will find Christopher and inform him the duel is off."

"Not so fast, Miss Cooper. I did not issue the challenge and nothing has changed as to why your brother called me out."

"I don't understand. Julia is going to be too far from Christopher's reach and you agreed to wait for the complete payment for the markers...."

"A gentleman doesn't hold his family member accountable for what transpires during a friendly game of cards. Christopher should consider anything he feels he owes me as paid in full." He watched her like that panther he often reminded her of seeing at Bullock's Museum.

"Lord Leighton, I do not understand what you are saying although I am grateful for your benevolence. That being said, Christopher will pay you everything you are owed plus interest. It may not be quickly but he will pay."

"Even to his brother-in-law?"

Struck dumb, Penelope tried to focus on his words but was confused.

"Penelope, I don't think you are understanding. Your brother will not call off the duel and after what he saw, after how I treated you, I do not blame him one wit. I would have done much more to any man who dared treat Margaret in such a manner. Offer the offences I offered you."

She began backing towards the closed door trying to judge how far she was to the hall and freedom. Feeling once she made the more populace part of the house, he would have to allow her to leave unmolested.

"Penelope, do not leave until we are done speaking with one another. If you wish to save your brother's life, we need to come to an agreement. One you may not be comfortable with. One you would fight, if it were presented in any other manner. I am asking for your hand in marriage. We will marry before the end of the year. Before Christopher can react in any adverse manner." He stood as if holding his breath.

Thoughts swirled through her mind. This would allow Christopher a new start, a new beginning with Lord Leighton's help as he once promised. It would be a way to put an end to the duel without either side backing down. It gave her a chance to be close to the man she feared she felt too strong of feelings toward. A man who had meant to demean her while making her heart beat faster with his every touch, his every glance.

"You haven't given this much thought, my lord. The talk, if there is any, will soon be forgotten. No one knows what happened while we were alone and Christopher wouldn't spread his thoughts on the matter, I promise you."

His head was shaking slowly from left to right and back again. "That will not do. Not to appease your brother and not to appease my own sense of honor. I treated you in the manner no gentleman treats a lady. I said things to you that no gentleman says to a lady. I owe you no less than marriage for my behavior."

Panicking because if anything would bring Christopher and this man into agreeing it would be that her good name needed the protection a husband could provide. "I don't think that is necessary, my lord, I truly don't. Ah, hardly anyone knows of our being together without a chaperone...."

"Except for my entire family and staff, you mean? And I intend to confess my full sins to anyone willing to listen."

She was flummoxed. "Why would you do so? Why would you say such things against me?"

He was close enough to touch her now and he reached out putting a hand on each of her arms. "Because I am the biggest fool you or anyone else could find. What

I thought was a way to drive your brother out of London also would take you from my side – just as I found a woman I could love and cherish the rest of my life." He stepped closer, to within a few inches of her body.

Her heart pounded in her ears and she wasn't sure whether to believe his words or his previous actions. She knew he desired her. He couldn't fake that even with an innocent as she was when it came to men. "I don't have to…."

"You do, you know. And I want you to. Now may I have your positive answer so that I can kiss you as your betrothed instead of a lecherous peer." His smile softened the hard planes of his face and he appeared much younger than at any other time.

"Do you think it the right thing to do? If you thought Christopher not good enough for Julia why don't you think as badly of me?"

"Because you have never held back your opinion of my life style, my views. I find I agree with some of what you say and think together we can bring the plight of these poor people to the attention of those who can help them all."

She stood unable to believe there was hope for her to make a life with this man and that he, in some mystical way, believed as she did. Could she accept his offer and make a good life for them both? "I think…."

"Don't think. Feel. It is your emotional depth that attracted me the first time we met. First your love and care for your brother and then that little flower girl. Soon after that I learned of how much you do to keep the schools your father started going, the personal hardships you live with so others will have something."

"That hardly warrants a marriage offer, my lord."

He pushed against her hips with his own, bringing her gaze suddenly up to meet his. "I thought I had made my desire more than obvious. Those words, those sensations, all those emotions in me wanted you, just you." He bent his head and covered her mouth with his holding her to his body with both his arms. He raised his head slightly allowing her to escape him if she wished, but she knew she was exactly where she wanted, no needed, to be.

Penny was so anxious to believe him. Believe they could make a life together, but they were so different in stations. "I can't feel we would suit any better than Christopher and Julia. How can we make it work without love if you are so sure they won't with love?"

"It's not the so-called difference in station but in attitude, in life expectations. Julia is spoiled. I admit that as does her mother and Julia does not understand what she will be giving up marrying your brother. She has never had to ask the price of anything in her life that she wanted. Tell me that wouldn't change if she married your brother?"

She knew he told her only the truth. Christopher wasn't that aware of the economics of running a household, let alone the costs of a young wife and possibly children. That was her fault. Trying to make his life easy with no more than a few idle warnings about the budget. She allowed him to over-spend while she pinched pennies in other areas. That would need to change immediately no matter what happened between her and the marquess.

Calling him the marquess seemed silly since he still held her to him and she could feel his need pressed against her pliant body. "Are you sure there isn't some other way? If I tell Christopher he has to wait, but then I seem to accept you… It will appear as if I put my wants over his."

"Then you agree you want me, too?" He kissed her mouth then continued. "There is the fact that as a family member he will have much more chance of seeing Julia than he would as a past acquaintance. He could visit my country estate where Julia and Margaret usually live along with Aunt Elizabeth."

She couldn't help herself. "There really is an Aunt Elizabeth?"

Chuckling and rocking her, he admitted, "Yes, but she retires very early in the evenings and I knew she'd not be awake to chaperone our dinner."

"Well, at least it wasn't a complete lie." She felt much safer and even a little cherished in his arms. "Do you really think this the best way? I hate to have you feel trapped or I don't know…."

"I am not the one trapped, my dear. I sort of set you up for this by visiting you when I knew you to be alone and getting you into compromising positions. Like this one." Lowering his head again they kissed for several minutes.

Breathless, she allowed him to break-away before saying, "Will you be visiting me tonight?"

"I would like nothing better, but I will not take any more advantage of you than I am doing now. I will visit your bed once we are man and wife, when there is no doubt why we are together. I don't want to feel I pressured you into this. I want you to want to be my wife, to share my life."

"Then I should leave to find Christopher. Explain things."

"No, it was dangerous for you to come here in the first place with the weather as bad as it was. It hasn't gotten any better while we, um, talked." He kissed her forehead and set her from him.

Opening the door, he called out as he guided her down the passageway, "Benson, have someone show Miss Cooper upstairs and call Mary to attend to her needs. She will be staying the night as the family's guest. And set back dinner half an hour."

"Yes, my lord. Right this way, Miss Cooper." The tall thin man said without a hint of interest in his attitude, although Penny felt he was almost bursting with curiosity.

Mary met her at the top of the stairs and led her into an occupied room. "I believe you and Lady Julia are about the same size or enough so you may borrow her things." Mary glanced at Penny's damp curls springing around her head and the still damp skirts of her dress.

"I couldn't do that, Mary. Let's just do something with my hair and I'll take a tray upstairs instead of going down to dine."

"I do not think that is what his lordship wants, Miss. I know you have the same size foot so let's just see if…." The maid returned from a dressing room with a lovely blue dinner dress over her arms. "This may fit without alterations."

A voice from the door interrupted. "Try the rose colored one, Mary, it will look fabulous with her skin tone. Mama thought since I'm young and blond I can wear any pastel color, but the rose makes me look as if I have blood-shot eyes. It's never been worn due to that fact." Julia plunked down on the bed and look expectantly at Penny with a smile.

"Th-thank you, Lady Julia, but there is no reason to loan me anything. I was just saying I could eat in my room and then rest until the snow stops."

"What? And leave Uncle Daniel to announce your betrothal at dinner alone? He may drag us all up here to hear the happy news standing by your side." The young girl almost chirped with glee.

"I, ah, I didn't think he was telling anyone. I mean not so soon. I haven't even told Christopher."

The girl's exuberance flew away leaving her limp. "Christopher. I suppose you heard I have decided to go back home. I don't like London or the people here – except for Christopher and now you, of course. We plan on going home right after Christmas if the roads are clear."

"You don't wish to stay for the rest of the season? Are you sure you gave everyone a proper chance before making a decision like this?"

"My mother has only me to worry over. She had her first season at seventeen and met my father who was already over thirty. He was well titled and rich and they were married at the end of the season. I was born less than a year later and then my father was killed when he was thrown while on a hunt. Mama thinks my life should be the way hers was, as well. Not the part of my husband dying young, but everything else she thought perfect."

"But you don't see it that way? Because you met, Christopher?"

"I never thought it the way I wanted my life. I plan on marrying, but not to a man twice my age. I want someone who I hold in esteem, who has honor as well as ambition and better feelings for our fellow man."

"A-and Christopher is that to you?" Penny

wondered what her brother had done to make this young woman think so highly of him.

"As soon as he gets a seat in the House of Commons he will. That is what intrigued me from the first moment I heard him arguing with a friend about the plight of the poor. Christopher said that educating the populace was an important start, but that more opportunity needed to be available as well. And women needed more than the parish church's help to provide for children left orphans due to war or work deaths. He said soldiers were still going hungry after being discharged from duties years ago. Some with missing sight or limbs. He wanted to change all the inequities between the classes that needn't be there."

"My brother said all those things? Arguing for help for those people less blessed then he?" Penny had difficulty aligning her young brother, the one wishing for his own horse and new boots, with the man Julia was describing. All the time she thought Christopher hadn't been paying attention to their father or worse, denying those truths, he had been listening. Storing the information away to take out and examine when he could position himself to do something about it.

"I'm glad you shared this with me, Julia. Sometimes one is too close to see the truth. I will probably always see Christopher as my little brother while you see him as the man he has become."

Mary had waited patiently with the lovely rose dinner dress and under-slip. Penny removed her damp dress and underskirts before donning the frothy creation with the many ruffles around the hem and the lace at the scoop neck and puff sleeves. Her hair was once again brushed straight and braided then looped into an intricately appearing style. Julia brought out a ribbon matching the dress and that was added to the golden-brown hair before deciding they were ready to go down to dinner.

Dinner was subdued with no one meeting anyone else's gaze. Only Julia was animated and talking about the Christmas ball being held at the end of the week. Something Penny hadn't heard about until that moment. Was she to ignore it and assume they would wed afterward so the family wouldn't need to recognize her or Christopher?"

She was to Lord Leighton's right while his aunt was on his left. Then Julia with Lady Margaret at the other end of the table. Glancing up to see if she could tell his mood, she found him staring at her. The glare was softened when he smiled and took her hand in his.

"As you all know, I have asked this lovely lady to be my wife and she has agreed. Since I am of an age, thirty-two to be exact, I do not wish to waste another moment without her by my side. I suggest I use our annual Christmas Day Ball to announce the betrothal and the wedding to be held on the first day of the new year."

"That will be perfect, Uncle Daniel. I even know which of my gowns Penny can have since I won't have a need of them and it is too close to the holiday to have one made." Julia turned appearing chagrined. "I'm sorry, Penny, but Christopher said you wouldn't spend money on yourself, which made him feel all the worse for needing to dress in a way to attract political backers. I thought as long as they were there and…."

Taking pity on her soon-to-be niece and hopefully one-day sister-in-law, she said, "No, you are quiet right, Julia. I will need the right wardrobe and it doesn't seem as if I will be given the time to have them made."

For the first time Margaret spoke up. "Perhaps not for the Christmas ball, but certainly enough time for your wedding dress. I have some pull with a very good modiste and she will have your dress done on time."

That was as good as an acceptance of the betrothal and she thanked her sister-in-law-to-be while feeling a slight squeeze on her hand of affirmation from the man next to her.

The footmen began the dinner service and Penny relaxed enough to enjoy the meal while Aunt Elizabeth went over the family members who would need to be invited to the wedding. Margaret added a few others, friends who lived in the country, and Julia merely nodded as name after name was added to the mental list Margaret kept compiling.

After dinner, Daniel, as Penny now thought of him, stood when the ladies did, saying, "I won't sit in here and drink alone like a dolt. Perhaps Julia will play something while we wait for tea in the green parlor?"

As they crossed the hall there was a commotion in the foyer and Penny was taken back a few hours and blushed thinking her arrival must have been as interruptive as the one going on at that time. Then she recognized the heated words and the voice of her brother.

"I demand to see my sister, Miss Penelope Cooper, if she is here. Otherwise, I must speak with Lord Leighton immediately. Someone left a message with my servant that she was being held in this house."

Penny rushed forward before her brother could take a swipe at an innocent footman trying to protect the family from a supposed lunatic. "Christopher, I'm right here and am not being held here against my will." When she reached him, he calmed as his gaze searched her face then body for any injury. "I need to speak with you, but everything is settled and we are all safe."

He took in how she was dressed. "You look lovely, Penny. I always thought so but those drab brown and charcoal gray dresses did nothing for you. And you know what I thought of your spinster cap."

Seeing his gaze move to someone behind her and soften, she knew Julia was standing there with everyone else. "Christopher, you feel frozen through. Come in near the fire and have some tea. I can explain everything but right now know all will be well."

He expelled a deep sigh. "I believe you but I don't see how you think this is all going to go right. I couldn't even find Archie to be my second."

Lord Leighton finally got tired of everyone standing in his foyer. "You won't need a second but I need someone to walk your sister down the aisle at our wedding."

"Your wedding? You mean you and Penny...?" He was looking to her for confirmation.

"Yes, and as a member of the family you will, of course, be invited to family gatherings where everyone will be present," she said pointedly. She saw his gaze move to Julia before blushing red and smiling knowingly.

Daniel added, "And as a family member, I will feel obligated and proud to offer you my support when you make your run for the House."

They reached the green parlor just as the tea trolley did. Lady Margaret poured while Julia played the pianoforte and spoke with Christopher who stood behind her turning pages for her. Probably explaining everything Christopher missed that evening.

EPILOGUE

"There you are, Darling. I've been looking for you throughout this crush. I don't think we've ever had so many attend an annual Christmas ball before." Daniel walked up to his lovely wife dressed in the finest silk and lace, red from the top of her feathered hair piece to the tips of her satin and gemstone shoes. Her skin was flawless and glowing, her smile a perpetual decoration on her face.

"I was feeding our son. He thought he had waited long enough."

Disappointed because he loved spending time with the three of them when she fed Nathanial, he told her so. "I would have gone up with you…"

"Both host and hostess couldn't leave our own ball at the same time. What would people think?"

"That I was making love to my bride? After all, we haven't been married a full year yet so to all purposes we are still on our honeymoon." He touched her low on her back where he knew no one could see his hand.

"I think giving birth two months ago put an end to the honeymoon, dearest, but I too, find it difficult to believe how much has happened."

They watched the dancers swirl past in an exotic blur of color. "I'm sorry I missed the waltz but I love watching Julia and Christopher in one another's arms. They look so perfect together I find it difficult to believe we both thought them too young."

"He may be a member of parliament come the end of next year. The life of a nation in such young hands is a little frightening." He said the words but knew if all the hands were as thoughtful and empathetic as Christopher's then England was in as good a hand as possible.

"Julia joining me with the school gives me hope of its continued growth. Together they can change the world."

"So you keep reminding me."

"When I think of all the ways things last year could have gone…. She shook her head in wonder. "And yet I find myself married to a man I so admire and care for, I thank God and all the Christmas stars I prayed on."

"I love you, Penelope. Don't ever think this wasn't something I wanted very much."

"And I love you, my autocratic aristocrat. You will always be in my heart – along with our children."

"Children? As in plural? Are you trying to tell me something?" He knew he teased but loved the way the blush rose from beneath the top of her low neckline to the roots of her golden-brown hair.

"No, merely stating a forgone conclusion if you keep up the way you've been doing since your conjugal rights have been returned to you." She tried not to let the wide smile escape but he found her smiling at him anyway.

He knew he was smiling widely, too. "Yes, now I remember exactly why I wed you. You drive me to distraction and make me unable to think rationally until you've had your wicked way with me."

She turned to him with her mouth already open to say something outrageous but instead patted his shoulder as if lifting a piece of lint. "We'll see who wins this argument in bed tonight."

"Midnight can't come soon enough for me." Then he kissed her on the mouth while a few nearby guests applauded.

The Best Christmas Present

London 1810

CHAPTER ONE

How had it come to this? A man his age viewing a
room full of young ladies barely out of the schoolroom
with their hair in ringlets and dressed up to lure and
entice, looking like little girls in their mothers' clothes.
Yes, they were the white or pastel colors allowed on
virginal bodies, but some of them…my God, what were
their mothers' thinking, for he knew the girls themselves
hadn't been able to voice their opinions. Most of these
dresses showed too much sophistication to go with the
banal conversations he had to endure during the few
dances he had forced himself to undertake. He would not
put himself out for the livelier country jigs. So that left
him with the waltz which young ladies were not yet
allowed to partake the floor to dance and a few country
standbys.

He was about to call it a night. This bride hunting
wasn't for the faint-of-heart and he needed a glass of
something much stronger than the watered lemonade
served at Almac's. As he went to give his regrets to at
least one of the dance's patronesses present, a young lady
newly arrived caught his eye. She wasn't trussed up in a
gown too old for her nor was it so frilly and child-like as
to remind him of his age. This young lady knew what
suited her lithe figure, her graceful neck shown to
advantage and her small ears dotted with appropriately
sized diamond earbobs. She wore a diamond bracelet
over one of the elbow length satin gloves and she showed
just enough excitement at attending the prestigious dance
as to tell him this was her first time there.

Wondering who she was, he watched as she waited for a haranguing mother if not both parents to rush to her side and guide her toward any unmarried male who had the misfortune as to be without a partner for that dance. Instead she stood easily and smiled or acknowledged several of the other young ladies as they danced by with their prize of the moment.

He thought it boded well that the other ladies greeted her readily and did not show the usual jealousy or fear that she would somehow come between them and their then partner. It gave him time to return to analyzing what it was about her that he found so irresistible. She was tall and he always liked tall women probably due to the fact they were easy to dance with and make love to with his taller than average height. He had already acknowledged her slender neck which was also a draw for him since he found he liked to nibble on it while driving home in the evening. Her large blue eyes were expressive as were her lips which seemed to be in a perpetual smile. High cheek bones that led their way to making her heart shaped face one of the most attractive he had seen in years.

As she turned away, he wanted to see more of her even if his interest in her would be noted and perhaps remarked upon. Even if she had a protective mamma or papa within a few yards of her - he wanted to meet her. Speak with her to see if the charm she seemed to exude was real or merely a fancy he was weaving around the young lady.

Stepping up to her, he drew attention by merely being present by her side. She gave him one of those smiles he had seen directed to others on the dance floor and his heart did a little flip. Oh my God, was he actually looking at a debutante who would be able to make him take that fateful step? A debutante who would move him off center and actually have him ask for her hand? Begin his family as his mother and sister had been demanding was his duty ever since his father died five years ago? Was his bachelorhood doomed and was he freely acknowledging that it wasn't as traumatic as he feared it would be?

"Have we met, my lady? I seem to find your features very familiar."

Surprisingly she stopped swaying to the music bringing the full force of her smile to bear without a conscious thought, he would have sworn. "Oh, my lord, I doubt that for I have recently come to town for the season. Otherwise, I have spent all my time in the country."

Ignoring the fact, they should not be speaking since they hadn't been properly introduced, she gave no false sense of alarm as if forgetting good etiquette. Instead she looked him in the eye and again his heart fluttered, but he felt it fluttered due to something in his past. Some barely remembered time and place. As if this young lady was superimposed over another from another time, but he would have sworn he had never met her and she herself had told him she was newly to town. It must be something about her perfume or the music or even Almac's itself. He had attended functions here since he was a young man not much older than the woman in front of him.

Bowing he said, "Let me introduce myself. I am Winston Wright, Earl of Williamsburg, at your service." He picked up the hand she automatically raised for his salute and let his fingers remain longer than he should as he played with the opening at her pulse point. As he suspected, it was as rapid as a hare caught in a trap.

"May I have the next dance?" How brave of him since he had no idea if the dance was one, he knew. Her eyes followed his every move as she continued to smile and nodded although he thought she meant to say something as well.

"I must wait for my mother before I accept any dance requests, Lord Williamsburg. Mother feels since I do not know many people yet, it is best that she vets my partners." Then charmingly she blushed and raised her free hand to her lips explaining, "Not that Mother will have any reason to deny your request, my lord. It is simply that it is my first time here and she said…"

Chuckling he nodded, saying, "I understand. I have a sister and my mother was the same with her. Mother's push their daughters to attend these functions while at the same time hate to see their little ones grow up." He realized he still held her hand and allowed her to retrieve it and tuck it into the other one holding the de riguer lace fan.

The young lady's gaze seemed to search the crowd at the wide doorway where people gathered to meet the new arrivals. It often became impossible to move through if one got stopped behind a popular attendee. That was probably what happened to this young lady's mother since the older woman must also be her chaperone. If the music began before the girl's mother arrived, he would spend the opportunity talking which was a much better use of his time than prancing like a fool down a row of strangers.

Once more, the movement of the young lady by his side brought his attention back to her. She drew him without device or purpose. It was her simple enjoyment of the music and the dancing that made him smile as if she were the most diverting of partners. What was it about this young woman?

"Mother!" The young lady by his side called out as a matronly lady walked by, but it wasn't this woman's attention which she was trying to attract. Instead, it was directed at a woman who appeared to be a sister, older by a few years, of course, but surely not old enough to be this girl's mother. But he was wrong – in so many ways. The woman wearing the dark green of a woman of some years and experience moved toward them.

She too had the large blue eyes over high cheekbones tapering to a pointed chin. Had the same lips curled up at the corners in a perpetual smile, the same regal bearing of her head on the graceful neck and lithe figure belying the fact she must have given birth to this girl, at least. Her chestnut hair differed from her daughter's blond, but he found it as attractive.

Almost gratefully, the girl grabbed her mother's hand pulling her towards herself and in front of him. "Mother, my I present Lord Williamsburg? He was kind enough to keep me company after seeing that I was alone and feeling like a fish out of water."

The mother was much younger than he first thought, but there again was the feeling of *deja vous* that he had felt with the daughter. How did he know them? He racked his brain, but without a name to put to the face he was at a loss. The woman's dark eyes sparkled as the lady curtsied, "It is interesting is it not, my lord, to find ourselves back in the same place so many years apart?"

Her words were like a splash of cold water. The music began and he ignored the fact he had asked the younger woman to dance and instead stood almost stupefied. There was something about the mother that was familiar as well, and he went through all the sisters of friends he may have met throughout the years. Still no name came into play although he thought he may be getting warmer.

"There is your partner for this dance, Emily. Return here as soon as the music stops, please, dear."

Nodding, the young girl curtsied and left with the man too young to shave let alone be out looking for a wife in the marriage mart.

"Ah, I find I am at a disadvantage, my lady. You have my name, but I do not have yours…"

Expecting a blushing, gushing apology for such an occurrence, he instead was met with that little grin-like expression as she said, "Lady Trowbridge, the Dower Lady Trowbridge. My husband died a number of years ago and a nephew ascended to the title."

If he was to recognize the name he didn't. Not for her husband nor the nephew so that probably meant the family didn't keep a presence in London and their lands were too far to be noticed, probably nearer the northern borders although her accent was definitely London ton.

He seemed to get the feeling that she knew he was having difficulty in placing her or her husband and that she was taking some enjoyment from the fact. Why? Why would a complete stranger find his lack of knowledge such entertainment? What would it matter to her?

"Do I know you? I mean from before possibly when you first came to town?" he asked, feeling he was getting closer to the truth.

"I'm not sure we ever really knew one another, but you gave me my first kiss." That gamin grin was there and the sparkle in her eyes a sure sign she was enjoying every moment of this unveiling.

"Hmmm, was I any good back then or was it one of those quick touches of lips and then escaping as soon as I could?" Two could play at this game and he was finding he rather liked his opponent's gamesmanship even as it intrigued that male part of him, he thought unmovable. At least while hunting for a wife.

But this woman wasn't wife material – not any longer. She had been wed for years and had one daughter to show for it. One daughter who was in the marriage mart. This woman was to be a grandmother not a mother so that left him where? Watching her expression as she watched his.

He let out a low laugh. "I apologize for any immature actions or words on my part as I worked my way through my salad days. Please be lenient with your thoughts if not gentle. I still regret many of those youthful indiscretions."

Still grinning she chuckled. "There is nothing to apologize for, I assure you. I used that kiss as a standard up until my marriage." Her gaze searched his face as he tried to say something that wouldn't ruin the moment – for him. He liked to think this charming woman remembered him fondly if not well.

She seemed to relent her verbal torture. "Oh, now I have you blushing. Don't worry it was only a kiss given in the moonlight at the Standishes' ball. I was wearing my rose lace dress and you were in evening wear, your hair was shorter then, at least along the sides, and you smelled of tobacco and sandalwood. But I barely remember it now, although I believe it haunted my memory all summer long."

He stared at her then smiled realizing she was having him on. "I am glad to have given my lady such a tantalizing memory. I live to serve…" And he bowed low giving himself time to recover from the feelings, these unfamiliar feelings, that seemed to assail him when he was alone with this woman.

Another matron seemed to be approaching and he took this time to do as he had planned on doing in the first place. "My lady, I wish you and your daughter my best this season. I find Emily a refreshing young lady whom I am sure will take the season by storm." Bowing, he kissed her outstretched hand and left.

A brisk ride was what he needed. A slow-paced trot was all he could manage with so many early visitors to the park. The sun had brought out not only his need to blow out the cobwebs the past few days of rain had caused to build up, but his thoughts of a certain chestnut-haired beauty. Just as his frustration was driving him back to the stables, a tall stylish young lady caught his eye.

Dismounting, he caught up with Lady Emily and bowed as she came to a stop. "Oh, Lord Williamsburg, what a surprise to see you so early. Do you know Miss Waters?" The young lady next to her tittered as he bowed over her hand as well.

"My pleasure, Miss Waters." The now crimson faced miss was struck speechless.

He returned his attention to his target. "I often rise early. Has to do with the old and decrepit not wishing to waste any daylight before we pass to our maker."

Laughing as he meant her to, she replied, "I don't think that description could possibly be used to describe you, my lord. I believe you are teasing me to get me to tell you how opposite those words you are."

"I'm glad you think so, my lady. It is good that I am not yet too old to hear your words." He knew that would bring about the grin he enjoyed seeing as she refused to add to his jest.

Peering around, he didn't spy what he was looking for so asked boldly, "Your mother, Lady Trowbridge, isn't accompanying you?"

"No, Miss Waters and I came with a maid who we left sitting on a park bench while we walked. She is older and doesn't like to walk as far."

He was sure neither young ladies' parents knew that about the maid they sent as chaperone. Would he one day find himself in the same spot? Unknowingly allowing a daughter to pull the wool over his eyes? By then, his very aged and weak eyes?

Debating with himself, he finally decided to be the responsible one and said, "I can't get a decent ride with so many about. If you would allow me, I will walk with you until you return to your maid." Both young ladies readily agreed and he fell in between them talking and listening to what young ladies these days think is important.

Winston arrived late, but he did arrive even if it was only in time to hear the obligatory toasts to the happily married couple. As with weddings, the crowd covered all ages and both family and friends were present. Place him in the friend's category since his host had been at university with him although an upper classman. In fact, he had been Winston's dorm tutor and kept the older boys from bullying both him and Alex too much. Usually he would have found something he needed to do rather than attend such an event, but usually he wasn't on the hunt for a wife.

He took another glass of Champagne from a passing server and tried to remind himself why he had felt a wife was needed. At his ripe old age of nearly forty, he had to set up his nursery or become one of those old men trying to beget an heir on a twenty-something young thing. Some days, when faced with a group of debutantes, he felt that same way now. Had he ever been that young? And the pimply-faced boys were as bad. How did England ever rule the world if everyone started out like that?

A striking blond danced past and he knew it was Lady Emily without a doubt. No mistaking her beauty or grace. He gave a nod of acknowledgement and she gave him an elfin grin. So where was the mother? He couldn't believe the one was here while not the other.

There. Just going out through the open balcony doors at the end of the room. She must have been here all along, but he had spent his time in the card room believing there would be no one to bother conversing with on the dance floor. All the same young ladies he had seen and discarded as potential wives earlier in the season.

Scanning the lighted garden, she seemed to be searching for something – or someone. Was there another man she had come out to meet with? Was she already involved in a liaison? Was he too late to make an offer or enjoy a night, a week, a month in her arms before he must pick from those debutantes he willingly left in the ballroom?

Unable to prevent the sound of jealousy to sneak

into his voice he asked, "Is there someone I could perhaps help you find, Lady Trowbridge?"

Seemingly unfazed, she blessed him with a smile. "No one I must find since I'm sure they will be busy."

Feeling relieved since she seemed to be looking for more than a lone man, he offered his aid. "I see a couple near the far end. I do not recognize them, but I fear they are not behaving as a married couple."

Again, that grin as she arched her neck trying to see what he could with his greater height. "Are you sure? I was trying to find our hosts to say goodbye. This ball is in celebration of twenty years of wedded bliss. I wouldn't put it past Sylvia…"

"Ah, that is not our host unless he has grown a full head of hair in the last fifteen minutes."

Sighing, she shrugged. "Then I will have to leave without giving them my best wishes although they are one couple who do not seem to need them."

Turning, she began moving towards the ballroom.

"Wait! We can't waste this beautiful moonlight and private moment. When will another opportunity happen for us?" Pulling her into his arms he didn't think - only felt and she felt so right. The right height, the right soft curves, the right lips as his closed over hers. Then he remembered – that first kiss and it hadn't been at the Standish's ball.

Their lips continued to meet and tongues entered and retreated sealing their bodies together in the prelude to a more intimate joining. He knew it and he could tell she felt it. They would become lovers and to hell with needing a bride or heirs or anything, but the feel of this woman in his life, in his bed.

Pulling away, her fingers went gently over her lips.

Not to wipe the taste of him away, but to seal it to her. Wide-eyed she shook her head as if in denial then turned and hurried through the still open French doors. He stood as if transfixed remembering the taste of her, the scent of her and remembered. Remembered another balcony where he had done so much more than kiss her.

CHAPTER TWO

"Mother, which of these dresses should I wear to the Thompson's recital? I've worn them both, but I think there will be less people tonight that saw me in it than this other." She held up the other one shaking her head. "Although I do think the blue brings out my eye color… Which should I choose?"

Half thinking about something she promised herself last night that she would never think of again, Malinda replied, "The white lace but add a blue ribbon under the bodice and woven through your hair. That way many won't even know it is the same dress at all."

"I knew you would know the right way to go on. I am so glad I have you with me instead of Aunt Edith. I don't think she would have wanted to attend half the functions you've taken me to. Thank you for disrupting your life for me. I do appreciate it even if I am having too much fun to show it." She hugged her mother one armed as she kept from crushing the dress hung over the other.

Malinda had a difficult time not telling her daughter she didn't really feel like going out that evening. Although, to be honest, the chance of a bachelor on the lookout for a bride wasting an evening going to such a small function was probably small. Coming to that conclusion, she felt better about attending. She enjoyed music, even badly played music which she was sure to hear this evening, and would rest easily among the other matrons proudly sitting there while their offspring showed off their talent. At least Emily played the pianoforte excellently and Malinda wouldn't need to hide behind her fan.

Wearing a gown she had worn before, Malinda greeted and was greeted by other parents, mostly mothers, who had accepted the opportunity to have their daughters in the spotlight of the ton. As she peered around, she allowed herself to breathe easier since most of the men present were fathers or older. Men too poor of hearing to notice the sour notes of a voice still changing or a misplaced finger on a keyboard.

She took the time to admire the artwork ornately framed along the music room walls. Some seemed out of place such as the pans frolicking with half-dressed maidens their intentions very plainly painted on their long-nosed faces. These she walked past quickly only to run into a large bulk of a man studying one in depth. Damnation, now how did she greet a man she allowed to kiss her so thoroughly just last night?

"Why, Lady Trowbridge, how charming to have run into you. I suppose your daughter will be performing tonight?" His expression told her he hadn't come to hear the amateurish attempts at entertaining, but for this moment. The moment she was forced to face him after that devastating kiss – because it had been devastating and had brought back all the reasons she had haunted the balls and assemblies when they were both young and foolish.

There she admitted it, at least to herself. She had been foolish in the past for thinking a man like Winston Wright would seriously think her a contender for his name. A man-boy who had so many other things on his mind that a girl he kissed in the garden didn't stand a

94

chance of being remembered once he had another in his arms. And she was sure there had been others. In fact, had seen him kiss another the same night she thought that he was the one. The one who would ask for her hand by the end of the season.

He was the reason she cut her season short, went home in despair and then was available to Lord Trowbridge when he called upon her parents looking for a wife who wouldn't mind being buried in the countryside. Her parents were thrilled finding an earl for her and she didn't care what happened to her once she came to realize that Winston hadn't wanted her in the same way she had wanted him.

He spoke first, "I know the kiss between us was something not to be forgotten, but at least we should be able to talk to one another. I came tonight specifically to talk about it." He appeared serious, but she couldn't face the man whose very presence shook her world to the foundation. His very look sent more than goosebumps over her skin and she feared someone with any experience with sexual tension would be able to read what was going on between them.

It wasn't as if she hadn't heard the talk and rumors. That Lord Williamsburg, who made it evident he had been looking for a wife was now sniffing around the Trowbridge chit. Did the man think she would condone his behavior? That his title would make her look the other way? Accept an offer for a slip on her shoulder while he contemplated marrying her daughter or, at the very least, another young woman of the same age? What hubris the man had. How so like him to think his wants and wishes would be enough for her to ignore what he was doing while he pursued a young wife.

"The kiss was a pleasant reminder of why I married Lord Trowbridge. I thank you for setting me free of those few childish memories I kept all these years. It made me thankful my husband found me in time so that I didn't make any further mistakes." She leaned in as if she were studying the painter's technique then finished, "I hope you do the same, my lord. We were not right before and we are not right together now. And you are certainly not the man for my daughter."

Winston seemed perplexed by her words, but she was sure he would figure them out by the end of the evening. Emily Trowbridge wasn't the right wife for a man like him. He would expect his wife to live where he told her to live, go where he told her to go, and ignore the talk of the ton as he kept mistresses and lady friends to his heart's delight. No, that would not be Emily's fare just as Malinda made sure it hadn't been hers.

He bowed as she moved on not seeing the portraits of people garbed in the clothing of the past century. Not family members, Malinda was sure, but worthy of purchase and exhibiting. People long dead and gone and without family members wanting to display them in their homes.

Her hostess called everyone's attention toward the semi-circle of chairs set out for the performances and Malinda searched for Emily so they could sit together. She didn't see Lord Williamsburg for the rest of the evening and she finally realized he had left right after their short talk.

"Mother, look at this beautiful bouquet that just arrived." Emily walked in carrying a very large and obviously expensive crystal vase of flowers.

96

Wondering whose eye her daughter had caught, she asked the inevitable, "Who are they from?" She hoped it was someone respectable because she could already see something in her daughter's eyes that meant she was intrigued by the sender.

"Lord Williamsburg - and they are for you. My, my, mother. You seem to have an admirer."

Feeling the blush rush to her face, she began to deny the possibility for so many reasons when she stopped and realized the flowers were proof of something going on between her and the man so why fight it? "I'm sure he thinks this is the way to your heart, my dear. After all he must compete against all those younger men."

"Mother, the man is older than you. How can he seriously think I would want to marry someone like him?" Her daughter may have said it bluntly, but it was evidently how she felt. What would Winston think if he heard it said so plainly?

"Lord Williamsburg is younger than your father was when we married. I can understand his need to marry a young woman who can give him the heirs he feels he needs now that he is of a certain age."

"Yes, but Father loved you. That is all fine for others, but I know what a marriage between people with such a gap in ages means." Looking at her, Emily continued, "Not that you and Father weren't happy, but his illness and inability to travel left you without much choice as to what you could do. I know you said you were happy and for the most part I believe it to be true, but I saw you in the garden sometimes and I thought you were lonely. That you had thought life would have more to offer than it did."

"I was happy with your father. You are never to

doubt that, but, yes, I think everyone feels bored with one's life. One wonders about the path not taken. I sometimes wonder that your father might not have felt happier alone with his botany studies and drawings. The meals he would not have bothered taking if left on his own."

"And that is exactly why I felt you two were good for one another. You gave father more to his life than he would have had otherwise."

Patting the chair next to her for her daughter to join her, she told the girl seriously, "But he doted on you, Emily. He said you were his one accomplishment in life. More important than any literary achievement or scientific awards he may have earned."

They both kept their thoughts as they stared at the flowers sitting on the table in front of them. "I still think Lord Williamsburg has a tendre for you, Mother. I've caught him watching you when he thinks no one else is paying attention. It's as if... I don't know. Kind of like he wished things were different." Glancing back at the flowers she said, "Perhaps this is his way of beginning over. You know, meeting you for the first time or like he wished you had met."

Emily didn't realize how close to the truth she might be. Not begin again as her daughter may imagine, but meet again as a widow and a gentleman. A gentleman who would be a very generous benefactor to her daughter and lover to Malinda. She did not doubt he had only gotten better, the kiss on the balcony was enough proof to know the man knew what he was doing in the kissing department. She could only imagine how well he did with the finer points of lovemaking.

Knowing there was a card tucked into the blooms

and knowing her daughter must have read it to know who the flowers were from, Malinda asked, "You're sure these are for me?"

"Certainly, your name was plainly on the front of the card with his on the other side."

"Well, they are probably his apology for last evening. We had a discussion about art in which we disagreed. He has evidently come around to my way of thinking." She fingered a velvety petal of one white flower then regretfully said, "Why don't we set them in the foyer. Their scent will waft through the house as anyone passes."

If Emily felt the request strange, she didn't say so, but merely picked the vase up and took it with her, the sweet scent of the gardenias leaving a trail if Malinda wished to follow.

CHAPTER THREE

"Am I still *persona non-gratis*?" The familiar voice was accompanied by the warmth of breath against her neck left bare by the ball dress.

"Lord Williamsburg, you are always a charming companion at any function of which I attend." She hoped her expression held the coolness she desired. One of polite acknowledgement, but not one inviting more personal conversation.

Sighing loudly, he looked down at his shoes. "I had hoped the flowers would have been accepted as I meant them to be considered. My most sincere apology although I feared your daughter would read the card so tried to keep it nondescript."

"I appreciate the thought although there is nothing to keep from my daughter. I do not plan on furthering our acquaintance on any level. Your interest in my daughter has raised her consequence within the ton, but as you and I both know, that will lead nowhere."

His next words surprised her and made her stumble as she went to move away from him. Anything to put some space between the two of them whether alone or in a crowded room. "Of course, she and I could never make a marriage work. She would always remind me of you."

Glad that he agreed with her, yet flummoxed at the reason why, she still looked for someone to rescue her from this conversation. Everyone she had a passing relationship with seemed to be on the other side of the room and of no help to extricate her from this man's presence.

"Remind you of me? Do you mean when I was that age? Many say we are similar, but I didn't know it was that strong. She has her father's coloring." His words were disturbing, but for another reason. Was he telling her that he was only drawn to Emily because she reminded him of herself at that age?

"Not in that way although I knew there was something about her that stirred me right from the first. It was the similarities to you. Even now as a grown woman you still have that same gamin quality about you. Once I saw you, I was drawn to you. I want us to begin again as if it were eighteen years ago. As if we were both young and carefree without the world's demands on us dragging us down."

"I don't know about you, my lord, but I wouldn't change the past years of my life for anything. I married a man I respected and admired, I bore him a daughter whom I love dearly and I cannot wait to be a grandmother within a few years. I feel sad for you if you regret past mistakes, but do not place me in those same regrets for, I have none." She was glad she could tell the truth so easily. It was freeing to admit she had been faithful without feeling she had missed out on something.

"Then come home with me. You have nothing holding you back now that we've found one another again. I promise there was something between us and if you're honest with yourself you would admit it, also. You knew me immediately, even after all those years. Let me show you what it would have been like - what it could be like between us."

"I will not miss what I've never known. I was never a woman who looked outside her marriage for

101

entertainment or relief of boredom. Why should I do so now?"

"Because, before we were both too young and too inexperienced to know what we had found with one another. Then you disappeared so suddenly. I became distracted with the rest of the season and hunting trips with school mates…"

"Yes, life interrupted us and possibly it was as it was meant to be. Look at you. You're what, nine and thirty? And still trying to find a reason to postpone setting up your nursery. Asking me to be your what? Mistress? Bed sport?" Shaking her head, she continued reminding herself as much as him. "I married a man I grew to love. He was kind and intelligent and grateful – grateful that I would marry him and give him a chance at a normal life. Something he had worried he would never get."

Unable to face the pity which often accompanied her telling anyone about her life and husband, she turned away. "Timothy had always been sickly. A word his mother used to mean he was often at death's door from various illnesses. He was at his strongest the summer I met him and I found him gentle and honest and funny. For a man facing death so often, he had a wicked sense of humor which kept me entertained. The first year was normal, I felt, for a newly married couple. I got with child almost immediately which raised his mother's hopes for an heir. She wasn't displeased with Emily since there was always next time. Only there wasn't."

The feeling of being disloyal speaking of such personal things didn't assail her as she thought it would so she continued. She wanted Winston to know what her life had been - what the path chosen was like.

"Timothy found himself unable to perform, to fulfill

his husbandly duties. I told him that I wouldn't miss that part of our life since I had Emily and him which were enough. He offered to look the other way if I found someone, a man, to whom I was attracted, but there wasn't. I knew then there never would be, not as long as Timothy lived. I should have made some other pledge because he died without ever regaining that part of his function leaving Emily an only child."

"I'm sorry your life, his life was cut short. I really am. He sounds like the perfect man for you otherwise and he gave you a perfect daughter."

Wiping a tear from her eye, she smiled, "Quit trying to turn me up sweet. I haven't made up my mind as to whether to sleep with you or not."

Hearing the hitch in his breathing brought her gaze up to meet his seeing such longing she had to turn away or face a scandal. She knew right then she would sleep with this man and damn the consequences. The thought of what it would do to Emily's chances the only force keeping her feet on the ground and her hands to herself.

"I'll do anything you wish, Malinda. Keep such tight control of myself no one else would ever know, ever guess. Please, give me a chance to make it right between us. Give us both the chance to know what this feeling is between us. What it should have grown into if given the opportunity. As adults, we can put a name to it. We can be closer than lovers ever are."

Catching her bottom lip between her teeth, she tried not to cry out her answer. Tried to keep the joy of being able to take this man into her arms and make love to him as she had fantasized all those years ago. "Yes, I will make love with you. I will become your mistress."

Touching the back of her dress so that others could

not see, she felt the heat of his hand. She leaned back against him and felt his erection firm against her fanny and took delight in knowing she had that effect on him.

"You don't know how happy your words make me, my darling," he whispered into her ear nuzzling it, the warm breath gliding over it.

"I think I do, actually." She allowed herself to turn enough to catch his gaze and they both chuckled.

"I will send a carriage for you to visit me. How and where will be up to you. I know you'll not want Emily to know, but please, don't keep me in this misery for too much longer." She could tell he wanted to kiss her and she wanted to kiss him. To seal their troth and let the other know of their commitment to their new relationship. She would be this man's lover and he would be hers.

Forcing herself to step away before their time together was noted by others, she smiled, fanning her face delicately while curtsying. "My lord, I thank you for the information and will look into visiting the museum myself soon." Then sailed away at a pace she hoped would not draw attention to where or with whom she had been speaking.

Malinda's hand shook as she moved one of the pearl studded pins from one curl to another while studying herself in the mirror. She saw her daughter enter the room and do a pirouette showing off her new ensemble. Malinda felt guilty for using the new purchase as a reason her daughter would want to attend the Ferguson's ball without her mother that evening. Instead, Malinda had begged off as chaperone and was allowing Emily to attend with another debutante and that girl's parents who explained they wouldn't be home till the early hours of the morning since the Fergusons were particular friends and this was their daughter Lucy's come-out ball.

Malinda had no hesitation as to allowing her daughter as much time as she needed. Malinda hoped to be otherwise engaged and her body had been humming with anticipation for the last four hours. Longer if she were honest with herself which she was tending not to be the closer she got to the set time for the carriage to be outside her house. She had never done anything half this delicious before and had thrown caution to the wind if all was said and done.

"You look perfect, Emily. Even the young Miss Ferguson won't hold a candle to you. Have fun and stay out as late as you wish. The season is dying down and you may as well enjoy everything you can of what is left of it."

"I plan on doing so. How foolish I feel when I think of how I argued about having a season, Mother. I will be much more prepared next year and hopefully the boys will be more mature. I can't see myself marrying any of the young men I've met so far."

Unable to stop herself, she asked, "What of the older men looking for wives. Men like Lord Williamsburg?"

"Oh, I suppose he would be someone's idea of perfect, but I want more than a title looking for a brood mare…"

"Emily! How you talk. Please do not say you have said such things in front of anyone else?" Although she was secretly glad her daughter wasn't in line to tie herself to a man looking for a wife only for the sake of bearing him children.

"I only say such things to you because we have

always been so honest with one another. Besides, I wanted you to know there isn't anyone I found so exciting I would change my life for one of being that man's wife. You keep me too happy and spoiled. Why would I give that up?" She jumped away from the hand Malinda tried to swat her daughter's fanny with.

"You look lovely and I'll see you at breakfast tomorrow. Now find your cloak and be waiting in the foyer. I'm sure the Hathaway's driver won't want to keep the horses waiting in this cold weather."

"One of the first things you taught me, Mamma, was not to keep the horses waiting in the cold," her daughter sing-songed as she whirled through the doorway and down the steps.

One last long look at herself and she was settled. She wasn't that young innocent virgin of all so long ago, but she was finally going to consummate her relationship with Winston. Take the place in his life, in his bed that she had pretended she never wanted. All these years and she had secretly yearned for just this moment. She heard the door open and the few words spoken to the footman and Emily was safely and securely off for the evening. That left only getting herself ready to leave.

Shaking out her fur-lined cloak, she hurried down the stairs. She didn't wish to keep the horses standing either, plus, she was very excited to be going to a rendezvous with a man she thought lost to her over a decade ago. A man whose thoughts as to his very existence had been banned from her mind. A man, though alive, had haunted her and her memories of her season for the past eighteen years.

CHAPTER FOUR

The carriage pulled up to the front of a narrow townhouse which looked much like the others on both sides of the block. Not seeing any numbers, Malinda had to trust in the driver knowing where he was going. The footman who came out and asked, "My lady, may I help you down?" gave some credence to this being the right place.

Winston was just inside the door and enveloped her in his arms barely before the door closed as the footman melted quietly away. She allowed herself this unaccustomed warmth and show of affection. How long had it been since a man's arms made their way around her? Since Timothy's last healthy spell? Since his funeral? Yes, that was it but now was not the time to think of such things. This was not a time to think of endings, but a time to think of beginnings – or rebirths. Time to reach for and grasp what should have been hers so long ago.

"I was worried you would change your mind. I was worried you had talked yourself out of this." His words were interspersed with kisses and nibbles on her neck and eyelids and cheeks. She had never felt so cherished, so desired.

"I must confess that I had my misgivings…. After all, I need to think of my daughter's future and being found with a man who is not my husband may not be acceptable to her future husband's family." She smiled trying to make light of her fears, but they were real and she had thought about them. Then she ignored the warnings and continued her plans to meet Winston and make him her own – finally.

"We will be discrete and you must realize what London society accepts is much different than what may be acceptable in the country. After all, I am a bachelor and you a widow of long standing. No one would think anything if we were to go driving in Hyde Park or for ices at Günter's."

"Both are done during daylight hours and among other people. This," she waved her hand to include the darkened entrance room and hall, "this is much different."

Smiling as wide as she had ever seen him smile, he said, "But we couldn't do this in the park…" And he kissed her so long and thoroughly her knees weakened. "Or this." And he allowed his hand to ruck up her skirts so that he could stroke the bare thighs at the top of her stockings. "Or this." And he pressed into her showing how everything he had done so far had affected his body.

Malinda had found it all thrilling and desirable driving her wants and passions higher with each word - with each touch.

Picking her up in his arms, he allowed her to drop her cloak before placing her arms around his neck. He asked, "You aren't very hungry, are you?"

Knowing what he wanted to hear and seeing as it was the truth, she said, "No, I'm not hungry for food. I only desire you…"

Another long drugging kiss and he was carrying her up the stairs to a room that was definitely masculine in its decor. Dark furniture, deep maroon bed draperies and coverlet, a fire already burning in the fireplace. She allowed her feet to touch the carpet before smiling at his enthusiasm. She fed on looking at him with his disheveled hair and flush from carrying her to his room.

He began undoing the fastenings of her dress. His fingers trembling in his haste or his passion. "Let me," she told him knowing she had worn a dress easily gotten out of in case she was expected to do so on her own. How innocent she must seem not to know how to have an affair at her age.

He stepped back the better to watch as she dispensed with the dress and then more slowly the corset leaving her feeling exposed and vulnerable in her chamise and pantalettes. The pink stockings held up by pick ribbons almost forgotten. Smiling, he knelt down stroking her leg through the stocking before untying the ribbon and rolling it down lifting her shoe off followed by the silk stocking. Then he did the same to the other leg as she balanced on one foot holding his head to steady herself. He peered up at her, but did not stand.

Instead he kissed her inner thigh making her stomach quiver and her breathing increase. She could do nothing besides watch, mesmerized by his dark head against the paleness of her skin and his fingers so tantalizingly close to the opening of the pantalette at the juncture of her legs. How was she to do this with any sense of decorum at all? How was she to pretend this wasn't the most wonderous thing ever to happen to her? Another kiss and her knees trembled with the need to fold beneath her.

Standing, he lifted her and carried her to the bed, their mouths fused and their tongues dueling for control. She didn't care. She let him win. If this was war, she would gladly yield the field to him since he was the strongest of the two of them for sure.

Hungrily he watched her as he removed his clothes with speed, tearing each piece from his body and tossing it to the side without thought. She watched as each beautiful part of him was revealed to her and his beauty took her breath away. It literally made her stop in mid-breath he was so perfect in body. Proportioned, width of chest to muscled shoulders and arms, tapered waist and firm thighs to shapely calves. Even his feet were masculine, but not as masculine as the erection jutting proudly from the dark thatch of hair. He stood allowing her to peruse him knowing she was delighted with what she saw.

Timothy had been so much smaller – everywhere although it was unfair to compare the two men. She had made a vow not to do so since her husband had been sickly, his whole life. In fact, she had been taller than him and he had been very fine boned for a man. But she had made a vow and she pushed such thoughts from her mind.

Holding her arms out, Winston kneeled as he came onto the bed with her. "Do I hold up to the years?" He teasingly kissed her before making himself comfortable next to her. His hand cupped one rounded breast and she hoped he wasn't disappointed. Time was so hard on a woman's body. Especially one who had born a child. She hoped he would give her the benefit of that experience.

"Hmmm." His only sound as he sucked one nipple into his mouth and cupped the other. He seemed pleased and if that was merely him being polite then she would accept anything she could get.

The hand stroked her body and began a journey between her legs where only Timothy had ever been. She pushed the thought of her husband from her mind once more and tried to feel what she would have felt if this were happening to her eighteen years ago and her uneducated body was receiving this man into it for the first time, for her first time. She didn't need to wait long for he positioned himself above her, her legs splayed to allow his larger body room and he thrust into her penetrating her to the hilt.

This is how it should be. How it should always have been. But she wasn't as sure of herself back then or as sure of her desirability. Now she knew better, but too late. No, not too late for they could be like this whenever they wished. Once Emily was married, Malinda would be on her own and could live as she chose. Even choosing to marry a man who once people thought was wooing her daughter.

They both stayed unmoving for a moment and then he began. The thrusts she could barely keep up with although her body knew instinctively what it wanted, what they both needed her to do. His breathing became harsh as he expended energy and stamina on bringing here-to-now unknown feelings from deep inside her to the surface. Feelings she hadn't felt before, but which she knew were part of this lovemaking. Again, remembering the promise not to compare the two men in her life, she focused on what this one was making her feel.

It grew and spiraled outward from her inner core. A core so deep she had never known of its existence. Just when she thought she understood what it was, it changed, blossoming into a kaleidoscope of colors and lights. Flashes brighter than any fireworks display she had ever seen. And accompanied by an explosion of fissions bolting through her body and out to the furthest parts leaving her exhausted and fulfilled and tingling in places she never dreamt of feeling.

This, then, was making love. What Winston had promised her. What Winston had gone through must have been similar to her own. For he was left panting and a dead weight on top of her after having had her in every position two people could physically be in and still remain joined.

He folder his arms around her murmuring, "That was worth the wait…"

She accepted the words as a compliment and fell into sleep being woken by Winston asking, "Are you hungry? Should I ring for supper?"

Still sleepy and wanting him again, she smiled shaking her head. "Not for food." That was followed by a satisfying hungry growl which had him tasting and licking her neck, breasts and other body parts available to his ever-moving lips.

The next time she woke it was to see the mantle clock as she startled completely awake. "I must get dressed and leave." Stepping out of bed into the chill of the air since the fire had become merely embers, she tried to make shapes into pieces of her clothing. Picking up one and then another she dressed as he remained in bed watching. She could see he was trying to find the words to coax her back to his bed, but he knew she must leave. It had been part of her agreement to do this thing with him, have this affair. She must return home before Emily knew she had been out. It was all right for her daughter to know her mother went to different entertainments for the evening, but not to learn her mother was sleeping with a man - and who that man was.

Leaning back with his arm behind his head, he

promised, "Next time, we'll eat first, I promise. I can't have you fainting away from lack of nourishment."

"Hmm, it seems as if you're the one who expends all the energy. Perhaps I should bring us sustenance next time." She grinned and he became serious.

"Then there will be a next time? You promise?"

"Why wouldn't there be a next time?"

"I just thought perhaps… Never mind. I will check my calendar and find another time we can meet. I have a few afternoons off as well and we can meet at a little inn outside of London. We'd only run into other like-minded couples, I assure you."

For some reason his words made her feel dirty as if they were hiding more than an affair of two available adults. "I don't think…"

"No, you're right. Evening is best. We will learn to keep apart the rest of the time."

"What? Why?" She didn't understand what he was implying. She must truly be tired if she couldn't figure out what he was saying to her.

"You know how gossip travels. If any of the Matchmaking Mothers learn of our liaison then my goose is cooked. I won't be able to find a wife who will allow me to keep you as well. I will need to pretend to be besotted with my new bride, of course, for a few months, but then she'll be busy with her friends. I can find a little house for the two of us."

Her stomach lurched at the future as he painted it. "You're still going to find a wife among the debutantes?"

"I assume so. I still need a suitable wife to bear my children, but I don't think it will be long before we tire of one another. You know how little time married couples actually spend together. Men often have mistresses on the side."

She nodded as if she understood - as if she saw herself as one of those women other women looked down upon. A woman sometimes pitied for having to take second place and leftovers from the man in her life. She knew of them but she never saw herself as being one of them.

Without trying to make any semblance of her hair, she raced out of the room as if it were on fire. What in the world had she been thinking? That she could be this man's paramour? This man's bed-sport while he lived his life in the open with his wife, his suitable young wife?

No, that wasn't what she thought this would be. Had no interest in being that for this man. Sitting back and watching him marry another, live openly with another and raise their children together. No, that wasn't what she bargained for. She felt dirty and foolish and stupid for thinking she would be anything more than a quick roll in the hay. Isn't that a term used for women who waited around for their man? Well, that wouldn't be her.

CHAPTER FIVE

"I had the best time, Mother. Marcus Ferguson, the older brother of the debutante's whose come-out I attended and heir apparent of the title, is so handsome. I wish you could have met him."

Trying not to think about last night and the debacle it became, Malinda smiled trying to engage herself in her daughter's chatter. "Of course, he was. All older brothers of debutantes are gorgeous and the heir and rich…"

Giggling, Emily said, "No, Mother, Marcus really is all those things. Well, I assume he is or will be rich although his father appears rather robust to me. I think it would only be the two of us for a while…"

"Wait. What are you saying? What about just the two of you?" No, no, no, she must stop Emily from jumping into the fire too soon. She was too young to make up her mind on such a momentous decision.

"I was simply making sure you were listening, Mother. I have invited him and his sister along with their mother to tea today so they can meet you. Lucy wants me to come and stay a few weeks with her during the season's break over Christmas. I thought it sounded a good time to see how I feel about Marcus – and he about me although he swears, he has stronger feelings for me already."

"But you only met and we discussed this very thing. You agreed you were too young for this kind of a decision and I explained how it was with me. I should have stuck to having at least two seasons before making such a drastic…"

"I know and agree, Mother. I, we, won't do anything that cannot be undone without a scandal, but Marcus and I have known each other since I arrived. He's the one I spend so much time with between dances." Seeing her mother weakening, she added the words Malinda knew would sway her doubts. "No betrothal shall take place, I promise. And so will Marcus - only he wants an understanding. If I change my mind or decide I wish to wait to find someone more to my liking then we will part amicably."

"That sounds very mature of him, but…"

"He is very mature, Mother, and in the guards, but will never go off to war since he is an only son of an earl. His uncle is in the war office and that's where Marcus will end up. There or possibly as an ambassador."

"My, an officer, an earl and an ambassador. What kind of a mother would I be if I didn't allow you to find your footing with such an imminent match?"

Squealing, Emily jumped up from her chair and hugged her mother. "I knew you would understand. Now I must go upstairs and change clothes since we didn't set a time for tea. I assume it to be during morning visits this afternoon."

"If my attire passes muster, I'll stay down here and open mail while you select the perfect dress to receive them in." She watched as her daughter danced across the room and out into the hall. Had she ever been so young and full of hope?

Her mind went immediately to memories of her youth. Of the hope she had to make a match with one of the young men she had met at Almac's. One of the young men the other debutantes had passed over. Instead she fell in love with a selfish young man who turned into a selfish older man. But could she blame him? Hadn't he been honest – both times?

Had he ever offered her marriage? Had he ever indicated he was doing anything, besides biding his time? Eighteen years ago, his plans included balls, hunting trips and a few months on the continent. This time it included balls, hunting trips and, oh, yes, marriage to a biddable, suitable young bride. His wants hadn't changed - only the words – and those only slightly. What had changed was her. She had to find out why she wanted what wasn't available to her.

There was only a week or so left to the season before she would be able to return to her husband's home estate. His mother had passed so Malinda was the only one in the dower house. It would remain hers for years since the nephew who had taken over the title was very generous. In fact, the young man would have been what Timothy's son would have been like if they had been so blessed.

Only a couple more weeks and Emily could probably be convinced to return home before travelling to the Ferguson's country home to the south. Malinda didn't think she was included in the invitation. It sounded like something the two girls had thought up. Besides, she would feel better licking her wounds in private. She could stay out of Winston's way until she left town and allow the house to go back to the rental agent a few weeks early. She and Emily could have an early Christmas together at home and then Malinda would have plenty of time to get over her foolishness once again.

It would be like the Christmas after Timothy died. There had been no decorations other than a Christmas candle, no parties or guests. They had been living in the manor, of course. The servants received their gifts and Boxing Day, but it was all a very somber holiday, for the most part. Timothy was very well thought of and well liked among the staff. Everyone loved Timothy.

Perhaps being home, alone, this Christmas would be the best thing for Malinda. She would be able to find comfort in the country and the quiet life. Possibly she could remain so out of the stream of things she wouldn't even receive invitations to Christmas events. That would suit her mood very well. She simply didn't wish to celebrate anything at the moment.

CHAPTER SIX

A lamb bleated and romped over the mowed grass of the back garden in the rare December sunshine. She laughed despite her feeling so poorly. She had come outside in hope the crisp air would help. Malinda was missing Emily and still hadn't figured out how she was to pull this off. Not without causing a scandal.

She hadn't realized how much her daughter's plans with Marcus would work out so well for all of them. According to the letters from Emily, the two young people were very happy with one another. Had even asked if perhaps Emily could forgo the second part of the season altogether or remain with the Ferguson family as Lucy's friend and Marcus's intended. It gave Malinda a way out of having to show up in London ever again. A plan which sounded more and more appealing as the days passed.

She hadn't been sure if she should allow the young people that much time together, but Lady Ferguson had assured Malinda the young couple were behaving themselves. Emily shared a room with Lucy who had sworn she would allow no hanky-panky to occur. If only Malinda had had such a close friend, she wouldn't be in such a bind.

Watching the sheep all head over the ha-ha to flatter ground, Malinda wondered what had disturbed the usually docile creatures. Peering around, her heart dropped as she recognized the size and gait of the man coming toward her. If she remained where she was, where there were no benches or shade, perhaps he would say his piece and leave. Perhaps he had found his bride and thought to tell her in person rather than have Malinda stumble across the poor young thing when Malinda returned for the rest of the season.

Pulling her shawl tighter around her shoulders she steeled herself for the meeting. "Lord Williamsburg, you are very much out of your district, aren't you? Heading to Scotland, are you?" Her smile was in place and so was his although he seemed tired.

"I made the trek to see you. I heard Emily has selected a young man which means you are free of any chaperone duties." So, he thought she was free to continue with their arrangement? Or rather his arrangement. As usual, she had failed to understand where she fit in with his plans. As usual, she had made the mistake of thinking this man was honorable and a gentleman.

"Not quite, my lord. Unsurprisingly, gossip is in the wrong of things. Emily has an understanding with Marcus Ferguson, but there is not an engagement. Nor is one planned until, at least, the end of the season."

There, that should allow him to bow out nicely. After all, she would have duties to fill that would take up most of her time – if she dared return to London after the holiday. Let him think she was and then tell him she has thought better of any arrangement between them. That she worried of the possible consequences for Emily and her engagement if it were discovered.

He peered over the sheep which had circled and settled to eat now they had nothing to fear from the large man standing in their dining room. "I've missed you – us."

Knowing she blushed, he smiled and then sat next to

her on the lawn without worry about grass stains. Perhaps he didn't know about grass stains. Well his valet will let him know tonight when he sees those buff breeches. His gaze met hers and he said, "Not only us – but us. Talking, sharing stories and arguing or agreeing. I miss being a couple."

Shaking her head, Malinda said, "We were never a couple. Not even that night we spent together. I was under a misapprehension and you…you were being you. It was all planned out in your mind. I would wait in some little bungalow in an appropriate part of town while you and your bride lived in St. James, or perhaps, Mayfair.

She watched the sheep. Gazing anywhere but at him as he taunted her with his masculine good-looks and boyish grin. "I would wait for you to visit. Making sure to be ready each night in case you could give your wife the slip. My life would revolve around you and your wants and your needs…"

His brows came down. "Is that how I made it seem? That you would always be waiting on me?"

"Didn't you see it that way? Now, be honest. At least I have that to remember about you. You did not mislead me on purpose. I was the one not hearing what you were saying."

"I don't remember saying any of those things. Well, possibly about the house, but I thought you understood that meant that I would care for you, take care of you."

Lifting her hand and waving it wide, she asked, "Does it appear as if I need taking care of, my lord?"

He grimaced, then said, "I wanted to give you something since you were giving me such pleasure. I didn't want you to come back here or move in with Emily when she wed."

"Well, I'm not moving in with Emily, ever. But I won't be moving back to London, either, so you needn't feel guilty about me at all. And I won't need to feel badly for breaking some poor young woman's heart." She gazed into his eyes. "All brides expect their husband's love, Winston. No one deserves to marry a man already set on duping her, making her a person to pity or be made fun of by the ton. I won't be that woman and I won't help you make any woman into one."

"So, if I promise not to marry, then you will consider being my mistress?" Her heart sank as she turned away with the new knowledge Winston would never learn.

"No, I will never be your mistress or lover or whatever other unappealing position you have open in your life. Please show yourself out. There is a nice little inn a few miles down the road used by runaway couples on their way to Gretna Green. It's only ten-miles north of here."

He lifted her hand in his and she turned to gaze into his eyes. "Will you go with me? To Gretna Green, I mean. Will you marry me and put me out of my misery?"

Her heartbeats increased to a rapid rate and she felt dizzy. She fought to stay aware of her surroundings, of where he was and what was going on. "What have you heard? Why ask me such a thing? You were just talking about marrying one of the debutantes."

Watching him, trying to draw breath, his head shook in the negative. "I have not mentioned my taking a wife until just now. You have been chattering on with all sorts of suggestions and they all seem wrong to me. I want you. I should have known that nineteen years ago when I first kissed you – and it was not in the Standish's garden, by the way. It was at the Kerston's garden and I remember you being a very good kisser – for an amateur."

She couldn't smile or grin or answer his expression at all. Something awful was about to happen and she had no way of preventing it. Going onto her knees, she retched from the bottom of her being to the tips of her toes. Tossed up her accounts would have been telling it too lightly. How was she going to explain this away?

She felt a strong arm come around her stomach to help hold her up as weakness replaced the need to empty her gut. He pushed a clean handkerchief at her which she accepted trying to catch her breath and move away from the mess she made on the once pristine grass.

"I do apologize, my lord. I must have eaten something to give me the sickness. I should go inside and clean up. Please see yourself out." She sipped from the cup of tea by her side, rinsing the horrid taste from her mouth. She felt well enough now not to make a fool of herself again as she moved toward the house.

Grinning, he allowed her to stand on her own. "That is the second time you asked me to see myself off. I won't be doing that now."

"I am quite all right, my lord. I explained…"

"I heard, but I want you to explain what I felt. I know we had only been together that one night, but I'm pretty sure I knew your body, your scent and your responses to me as well as I know my own. Only yours has changed. You're with child and you needn't try to tell me it isn't mine. I also know when you are lying. You won't pull off such a Banbury tale to me."

"I, ah, I… Oh, Winston, can't you let it go? I won't say who the father is and no one will ever guess. We weren't seen together more than what I was seen with anyone else. I'll make sure people assume the father is local. Perhaps a man of lower class."

His face reddened. "Do you think I would not claim my own child? What kind of a man do you think me? And I had asked you to marry me before I knew you carried my child. Do you know what that cost me?"

"Cost you? In what way did it cost you?" She was beginning to become angry now that her embarrassment had eased.

He grabbed her to stop her progress toward the house where she was sure there were eager ears trying to hear what was going on. In quiet tones, he said, "We can do this here in what is little less than on public display or you will walk with me to look over the orchard where we can shout as loudly as we wish."

With a tight smile she said, "The orchard, my lord."

Helping her over the lumpier ground, he finally sat her on an abandoned crate while he sat on the grass very near her. So near he picked up one hand and played with her fingers while talking. "This is my child and I will acknowledge it fully."

"I, ah, that may interfere with you finding a wife as you had planned."

"Plans can be changed. In fact, I do so on a regular basis. In fact, they just changed this moment. I told you I wished to marry you, but I wasn't honest. I never told you why I hadn't asked you to marry me in the first place." He gazed into her eyes as she braced herself for his answer. "I thought you couldn't have a child at your age…"

"Why you, you, old coot! How old do you think, I am?"

"I know how old you are, but you have a daughter

who could become a mother herself."

"That doesn't have anything to do with it. I can bear children for the next several years. My mother was forty and two when she gave birth to me and her mother was forty and four when she bore my uncle."

"I'm, ah, sorry. I didn't even think to protect you when we…"

"I understand and I am to blame as well. I didn't think about such things because I never had to. After Emily, Timothy went into a decline and never recovered completely. He often had to be carried to his bed and we didn't, um, you know, after that."

His gaze seemed to soften. "How long ago was that? How long were you a wife without love and affection?"

"I always was loved and Timothy was rather romantic. He simply wasn't able to show me much physical love, but it didn't matter. I had Emily and I had a husband who cared deeply for both of us. He adored Emily and never felt cheated because she wasn't an heir. He said there was always a male relative somewhere who would be chosen."

Gazing over her head he said quietly, "I think I know what he meant. I don't think about this child as being my heir or not, but simply as mine. If there is only a girl for us then so be it. I'll love her as much as I love her mother." He kissed her before she could say anything and perhaps that was best. She loved this man and together they would make a family just as Emily would leave her and make her own with Marcus.

Finally, pushing himself from her as he tried to tuck at least one hand behind him to prevent another onslaught of passion, he explained, "We will be married by Christmas. The best present I can give myself. We can make love while the maid packs for you or we can make love in the carriage on the way to the border to get married or we can wait, impatiently, until it is legal and make love back here tomorrow. What is your choice?"

Knowing she was being naughty, but not caring, she replied, "Why not all three? I am already with child."

A broad smile crossed his face just before he covered hers with a shower of kisses. His response was everything she could have wanted, could have wished for. Her lover, her child's father wanted them both as much as any wedded husband, more than most. This was her very best Christmas present.

EPILOGUE

"Here, you need this more than I do. Winston handed a glass nearly topped over with good honest Scott whiskey to his friend, Tony, who came to give him company during Malinda's confinement. The gesture was nice, but he wanted to be with his wife not waiting in a room so far from her. Too far to hear anything that may be going on.

"Tony, if you would excuse me, I am going to where I feel I should be – with my wife. Damn etiquette or societal rules or whatever controls us during this time. I will be there by her side. She isn't young any longer and I fear this will be too much of a strain." He was already heading to the door as Tony began draining the glass.

As he approached the chamber they decided the baby would be born in, he heard Malinda's groan and then a moan of pain. Both sounds urged him to open the door, find the bed where she lay and ignore the other women's cries that he was not allowed inside the room.

Grasping his wife's hand, he said, "I will never put you through this again, I promise."

Perspiration showed on her forehead and she looked tired and pale. He hated himself for putting her in this condition. She was enough for him, had always been what he needed.

"You will think differently once our baby is born. I assure you. I am strong and this is no different than when I bore Emily." Another pain seemed to distract her from her thoughts. When it was over the midwife gave her steady words of approval.

"Possibly you are correct, but it doesn't feel that way right now. I want you out of pain and resting. I want you happy and content. I want my wife and then I will be happy and content."

"You have your wife and soon a child we will both adore and spoil. I only hope it will not be an only child for us. I always thought Emily would have been much happier with a sibling." She grimaced trying to hide the fact pain traveled through her body.

"One is enough. We don't need any more. You are dearer to me than an unknown child." He kissed her knuckles and gazed into her eyes. Saying a prayer that both his wife and child made it through this trying time.

"Oh-h-h-h…" Malinda's hand tightened on his as she lifted her upper torso to help her body push out the child.

The midwife became busy and called out, "It's a girl. A bonnie lass ye've got yerself."

"Another daughter, Malinda. We have a daughter." He was laughing as he felt tears enter his eyes. His wife was happy and smiling and he was happy as well. He had the family he wanted and the wife he always should have had. His heart was so full.

Malinda almost came off the mattress as she suffered through pains which appeared as bad as the birth. "What's wrong?" he called out to the midwife who had passed his daughter on to another woman who seemed to be bathing her.

"Let me see here. The after birth was already being flushed. I don'a,…ah-h-h, I see what we 'ave here. There's another bairn hiding 'hind the first. Let's see now."

Winston could barely contain himself with worry

that his wife wasn't through with the pain. He had to worry about another infant who may not make it into this world alive. "Malinda, dearest, please be strong enough to do this. Please don't leave me, us…"

A long groan and her hand squeezed his with more strength than he thought his wife possessed after already giving birth to one child.

"Aye, there he be, yer lordship. The boy be waitin' ta make an appearance, as they say." The old crone cackled with delight in birthing two babies. Both looked healthy with the first held quietly while his son bellowed loudly at being disturbed from his warm cocoon.

Joy, a word he never understood before, filled his heart and his body. He kissed his exhausted yet excited wife. "You have surpassed anything that would have been asked of you, my dearest, my love. You owe me nothing more. My life will be dedicated to you and our two children."

"I have but thirty and six years. If I follow my mother's family, I will have time for more."

"No, I will not see you in such pain again. In such danger of my losing you." He kissed the hand he still held.

"Husband, I do not think you wish to forego one of our favorite pastimes – do you?"

Remembering the lovemaking that brought these two into the world he chuckled, "Perhaps not, but we should be able to control ourselves so that there are a few years between them. Besides, twins must count for something."

"They do, dear husband, they most certainly do."

Sugar Plum Christmas

London, England 1807

CHAPTER ONE

The young gentleman wearing morning clothes picked up one of the petit eclairs Michie had placed on the silver tray covered by flower petals. Popping it into his mouth, he licked his fingers, saying, "I bet you are as sweet as that little bite of confection."

Pulling her to him tightly, he leaned her over the table so that she could feel his body against her backside. Knowing she couldn't cause a distraction this close to the main rooms already filling with guests, she tried to pull herself from beneath him.

"Sir, I am here to set-up the wedding breakfast and nothing more. Now leave me to get back to my work."

She could smell alcohol, not blue ruin, but a dangerous aphrodisiac to some men just the same.

He craned his neck to reach her face as she turned away still trying to pull his hands off her.

He kept up his assault. "Let me have a taste. I will make it worth your while. I promise and that is more than your other men probably give you."

"Leave the girl be, Ripley." The deep male voice sounded strong yet bored. As if finding this man, Ripley, was getting tiring. "Don't you have something else you need to see to?"

His words brought the desired affect Michie had been seeking. Her body was freed. She gasped for breath as she straightened the uniform she wore while at work. Embarrassed, she kept her gaze on the boxed confectionaries with the distinguishable symbol of Gunter's Tea Shop. Her fingers trembled as she picked up another eclair and set it in the row on the silver tray.

Knowing the second man was still present, she prayed he hadn't chased the younger one away only to replace him. Or to offer her some other proposition she would find as offensive. As someone working in the finer homes, this was not the first time some man had tried to opportune her.

The same dulcet tones inquired, "Do you need a moment?"

She took the chance to glance at him now that he didn't seem a threat. Tall and broad, but not untidy with it as the other had been. His sapphire-colored eyes were mesmerizing. She forced her gaze back to her work. "N-no, my lord. I need to finish these trays and begin on the ices as soon as the guests are seated."

"Time sensitive, to be sure. All right, then allow me to aid you. These biscuits, do they get lined up as well?"

Her eyes rose to meet those of the handsome gentleman seriously thinking of helping her fill the many trays left to be done. "Oh, my lord, you could get frosting on your fine clothing. I can get them done in time. I am quite recovered…ah, recovered from whatever happened." She felt the heat of a blush over her entire body. Perhaps that is what happens when one lies to someone who appears too perceptive.

"I have others and my valet can get any stain out." He went to pick-up a biscuit, but before he took the first one, she instructed, "You best take the eclairs and line them up, my lord. I'll take the biscuits. Those are to go in a pinwheel spiraling from the center outward."

He must have watched since she heard him say quietly, "I never appreciated what goes into traying up something that was going to be gobbled down by unappreciative hordes of mouths."

Unused to working beside a gentleman, Michie was not sure of the protocol "Wh-what, my lord? Were you speaking to me?"

"No, simply asking myself why I worried about any of this at all."

"I can place them all, my lord. You can return to whatever it was you were doing originally. I am grateful for your interceding on my behalf, but I am able to finish my job."

"Don't be concerned, I won't tell your supervisor of the dust-up. After all, it was one of my guests who was the cause of it all in the first place. Can't even arrive at a wedding breakfast sober. Probably still out and about from last evening." He sighed, "I understand the groom is in about the same condition."

He announced momentarily, "The tray is full and there are still two left in the box. Do we simply eat them?"

She glanced up to see if he was joking and found he didn't seem to be. "No, my lord, we begin a new tray, although technically, these belong to you. You can do whatever you wish."

"Hmmm, I find I wish to eat one."

She watched as he put the petit éclair into his mouth. Watched as his lips closed over it. A touch of chocolate sat on his top lip a moment before the tip of his tongue came out and licked it off. She noticed his eyes had been closed this whole time to ensure he wasn't interrupted in his gratification. She had never seen a man enjoy anything quite so thoroughly.

The other éclair went the same route.

"Um, there are several dozen more in the other

boxes, my lord, if you so desire."

Grinning, he said, "Oh, I so desire, although I do try to limit my hedonistic behavior this early in the day."

He pulled another box toward him and opened the lid showing rows of the small creations she had worked all night on. These he placed on more flower-petaled trays as he had been doing. They worked without comment for the next half-hour to find the boxes empty and the trays filled sitting on every flat surface in the large butler's pantry.

"There, that must be it, then." He dusted his hands and looked longingly at the neat rows of eclairs. She thought they must be his favorites and she agreed with him most days. There were times when other items became foremost on her taste buds, but today these were her favorites, too.

"Thank you, my lord. I hear the waiters gathering in the kitchen. They will be in for these trays any minute." Wiping her hands down her apron, she hoped the man would take the hint and leave before anyone else knew he had been in there with her. Already cringing at the questions that would be asked, she watched him closely.

A slight grin and tip of his head. "Are you giving me my conge?"

"Your what, my lord?"

Smiling, he shook his head. "I will return to my sister's side as she sees my niece married off – finally. It has been a long drawn out summer for all of us involved. This was something to begin the season. Draw all the ton families back to town. By the number out there, it seems Lady Margaret has a crush to be proud of." He bowed and Michie responded automatically with a curtsy.

She called to the waiters to begin carrying the trays

while she hurried to the molded ices waiting in wooden boxes filled with ice chunks surrounded by straw. Crystal dishes were set out and Michie filled them as quickly as possible sending more waiters with full trays out amongst the guests with the favored small spoons used to eat the indulgence.

An hour later, Michie collapsed in relief onto a bench in the servant's dining room. The dishes from Gunters were washed and dried ready to be packed-up for their return ride to the shop. All else belonged to the home owner. The kitchen staff, both regular and those brought in for the special event, were about to enjoy their tea. They could take their time since the family were dining elsewhere that evening.

"Micheline, come join us. You deserve a rest." She knew her smile was tired looking, but there wasn't much she could do about it. She had been awake and working since two in the morning.

"I would love to, Thomas, but I need to get everything back to Berkley Square. There is another event tomorrow night I am to work on. I need to catch some sleep before then."

She hated turning Thomas away. He had been friendly from the beginning and been a great help when she was first setting up in the large houses. As a female she had been ignored, at first. Thomas had told her to take over like a Colonel with his troops. Tell the household help what she needed, what she expected and then give orders. If she lost their respect or control, she would never get her desserts and pastries trayed and served properly.

Good-natured as always, he chirped, "Another time then. I'm scheduled to work the Foster's musical and the

Witherspoon's ball this week."

"Oh, I may see you at the ball, then. We are furnishing desserts for the midnight supper."

"As it sits now, I'm to slice the ham or possibly the game hens. So, we'll see one another?" Thomas was a nice young man, but Michie wasn't sure she should lead him on. She wasn't ready to get serious about anyone. She had plans to take the world by storm someday.

"You know how busy it gets at one of those things. I won't have time to socialize."

Noticing the entire staff was paying attention to Thomas and her personal conversation, she merely waved goodbye. She began carrying out the boxes of dishes to the waiting wagon.

Arriving at the shop by the back door, Michie began the unloading. Puddles formed under the wagon as the ice melted and dripped through the straw. The driver would be in charge of salvaging any ice still usable so that freed her to begin her real work inside.

The kitchen was still redolent of vanilla and lemon. The two flavors of cake she knew she would be frosting that evening. But first she needed to rest. Besides, the backrooms were still too warm to try to frost cakes. Looking in on the cakes cooling on the wire racks, she realized they hadn't been cut yet. Another hour added to her workload. Since they hadn't been cut into squares, then they hadn't had the first coating of melted lard and sugar applied, either.

Sighing, she made up the mixture which would seal the crumbs and freshness in while allowing the frosting she applied later to adhere. Slicing the cake, she made short work of what used to take her hours. She had to accept the fact not all the cake would get used. Only those perfectly shaped squares or circles were acceptable for frosting. Only those perfectly frosted squares and circles would then have a perfectly designed flower or marzipan perched on top.

She eyed the trestle bench and blanket, but sleep was still a long time away. She needed to frost while the room was at its coolest, before the baker came in and fed the wood ovens again.

Beating the lard with the sugar, she added a few drops of flavoring steering away from the vanilla seeds that brought their distinctive brown stain. Clear vanilla, distilled so the white frosting was kept pristine. She beat small batches to keep it fluffy and fresh as she buttered pieces of cake leaving enough to appear as if each had been dipped. Special food dye would be used in the frosting for the flowers. Pink for the vanilla cakes and saffron-yellow for the lemon. She only had a hundred of each so a few hours would see them done and in the boxes. Green leaves would be added to the vanilla cake then the yellow flower added to the lemon flavored once the frosting was set. Marzipan would be placed in the center of the heavily frosted circles. Perfect replicas of berries, pineapples, and peaches. Perfectly colored and flavored. These had been made earlier in the day by younger apprentices to the kitchens. The master baker oversaw their training just as he had hers.

Day was breaking and the rotund master baker arrived with his assistants. He was a loud man used to giving orders and being obeyed. As he barked his demands, others hopped to do his bidding. That included Michie who knew any chance of sleep was gone.

A hissed, "Micheline. Micheline, are you going to

139

be free tonight?"

Biting her lip to keep her hand steady as she added the final touches to the tiered cake with Chantilly cream, she finished before turning to her admirer. "Thomas, I told you I would be working tonight. I still need to finish the croquembouche as well as un-mold the crème bavarois. Now shoo."

The remembered dulcet tones of a few days before sent shivers down her spine. "Do I need to rescue you once again from a male's unwanted attentions?"

She saw Thomas dodge behind the door followed by the sound of his rapid steps as he sped away.

"Thank you, my lord, but Thomas is a friend. He sometimes works for the same company I do when we are busy. Gunter needs waiters to run the ices across the street to the carriages and customers from the park."

"Ah, yes, I have partaken of the famous ices myself."

She turned to the high tower made of round filled cream puffs. Looking at the selection of crystalized fruit in front of her, she began designing a pleasing work of art that would be torn asunder by the guests in a few hours. They would barely notice the beauty of it. Still, she would create the edible art as she knew her employer expected.

"So, you do this every evening? Create works of art, set out trays of comfits and delights?"

Trying to concentrate on the work in front of her as well as appear polite, she continued selecting the perfect piece of fruit for each empty area between the cream puffs on her tower. "Part of my job is to see to displaying our products to the public."

"Are you ever tempted to eat your creations? I mean,

before the guests get hold of it?"

She couldn't help the chuckle escaping, "No, my lord, not after the first hundred or so. The staff get to eat the unfortunate mistakes made by the bakers and decorators, but after a while it wears thin. After you've had so many, one becomes immune to their sirens' song."

She saw his head tip and a brow raise. "What an unusual way of phrasing that. Where are you from?"

Startled into remembering who she was at that moment, who everyone thought she was, she answered, "This side of Cheapside, my lord. I was able to read at the first place I worked before I apprenticed at Gunter's. I found the books very interesting and remember certain phrases, I guess." Her words had the desired effect although he continued the interrogation.

"Your accent isn't of Cheapside."

"You know how we all go on, my lord. I've been raised in many places along the way. My mum worked as a governess and some of it must have rubbed off." How to take back the words she used before? How to make this man leave before he gained too much information.

"My lord, I believe I hear a cotillion tuning up. The first dance of the evening. I'm sure someone is holding her dance card and fretting over not seeing you."

"Presumptuous of you to remind me, but correct, none the less." He made a slight bow. Smiling, he left through the hallway door.

Cyrus couldn't help but smile. He sniffed the fragrance of the biscuits he had pilfered from the box. Ah-h, almond. He loved the scent of almonds and these little delicacies were one of his favorites, as well.

That serving girl, no she was more than that. She had discussed the items in a proprietorial manner. As if she had handcrafted each and every one. Perhaps that was the truth of it. She had a hand, at least, in baking or making each dessert. He had tasted some of everything that had been presented at his niece's wedding breakfast. Had found all of it appealing and delicious.

Was that what had drawn him to the lower floor of his hosts home tonight? The fact he wanted a chance to see what delights awaited him at this evening's midnight supper? Or was it the opportunity to see and speak with the raven-haired, dark-eyed beauty from the wedding breakfast? To see if she was as she seemed with her rosebud lips and shy manner.

He had passed the wagon with Gunters' symbol on his way in. He became acutely aware she might be setting up the trays as she had at his home. Nothing short of seeing whether or not she was here would settle him. But why? He had never searched out a servant before, certainly not his type of thing to do. He wasn't, Ripley. There simply was something about the young woman which intrigued him. Possibly because he never had anything to do with a woman of ambition, not the kind this young woman had anyway.

He wondered if he could entice her to live in a house on Curzon Street. Would she settle for that or would she demand more for her time? Could he live with the idea she could provide for herself? Possibly leave him when she became bored or wanted to go to another protector? For some reason those thoughts made him uncomfortable. He would ponder those ideas at another time. Tonight, he had spoken with her and he was content she had an interest in him as well.

Licking the last of the finely ground sugar from his fingers, he continued towards the ballroom where his sister waited for his partnering. She would wait. She would have no idea what had kept him from her side so he was safe from sisterly inquisitiveness.

Cyrus chuckled quietly to himself. He had a hunger for some little tidbit of sugar and spice. However, he was no longer certain he was thinking about pastry.

Michie tugged the hooded cape tighter around her neck. The moonlight was non-existent and the streetlamps in this section of town few and far between. More to denote particular crossroads than to aid in pedestrians making their way home.

A night watchman came out of the shadows brandishing his baton. "Hey, you! Git yerself off a here. No place for likes of ye."

Startled, Michie tried to explain, "No, sir, I was just leaving work at a house…."

"I can guess whuts ye were doin' at one of 'em houses. Now be off wi' ye. I likes me streets clean and safe for those that live on 'em."

She scurried toward the end of her street. She wasn't going to bother telling the man she belonged there. The fact of the matter was, she didn't feel as if she belonged there. A squalid house on a squalid street where her mother and her shared a couple rooms on the second floor.

In her rush, she made more noise than usual getting the door unlocked. She hung her cape and removed her boots before going further into the house. The streets here were so filthy she hated thinking what she was dragging in with her.

"Michie? You are so late tonight, *ma cheri*. I thought you were staying at the bakery. That you had to change your schedule."

She went to the diminutive dark-haired woman and bent to kiss her cheek which felt warm to her. "*Non*, Maman, it took longer to get everything put away. If you are hungry, I've brought home some pigeon pie and a crab cake."

"Oh, you shouldn't have, Michie. What if you got caught?" She accepted the parcel with both hands.

"*Non*, the chef gave them to me. He gave some to the others as well. Said the master of the house refuses to eat food already served once."

Unfolding the delights wrapped in a cloth, her mother inhaled the savory aromas. "Well, the rich can well afford to have such finnicky behavior. I know from experience food is not something you can take for granted."

She watched as her mother re-wrapped the items and placed them in the area they treated as the kitchen. There was no stove, but it had a sink with a common drain and a cupboard holding the few dishes and flatware they possessed.

Smiling, her mother turned to her, "How was the ball? I take it there were beautiful dresses and jewels galore?"

"I am sure there was, Maman, but I do not get into that portion of the house. I did hear the orchestra playing and it was lovely. The chef grabbed the housekeeper and they waltzed, at least, that's what he called it. He's German so he should know."

"Yes, he should know, then. All the best waltz

composers are from there."

She followed her mother to the sofa. Evidently, she was rested enough to take time to talk and Michie could spare a few minutes of her time. After all, being away from home for ten and twelve hours at a time made a lonely existence for her mother. Michie knew the older woman still feared being recognized. Possibly sent back to France where she would face a trial.

"You should be attending these balls, Michie, not working at them. Gentlemen should be asking to have their names placed on your dance card. Not asking for more macarons."

"I no longer serve the public, Maman. I don't see people of society at all."

She studied her mother's black-hair and dark eyes set wide in her heart-shaped face. Michie knew she resembled her mother, especially her mother when she was young, and feared someone would recognize the similarities. Find her mother through Michie's ambition. Not serving the public as she had when she began working at Gunters was less stressful.

A pang of regret pieced her heart. She was keeping the gentleman a secret from her mother. She knew her mother would worry over the reason a gentleman would spend any time talking with a pastry baker. Someone little more than a servant. Even Michie hadn't come-up with a good reason the man spent so much time in her company. Or asked such personal questions about her living place and manner of speaking. It was another secret and Michie felt she held too many secrets from too many people already.

CHAPTER TWO

It was almost two o'clock in the morning and the party was still going strong although Michie's part was finished. The midnight supper was finally cleared-up. Michie had wrapped the last of the left-overs for the household and placed them in the pantry.

The sound of footsteps had her turning sharply. A soft cry escaping as a hand touched her shoulder.

The familiar dulcet tones. "Sorry, that was clumsy of me."

She faced the gentleman who had come to her rescue even when she hadn't needed it.

He continued giving her time to think before he said, "I thought if you were still working and it being so late, I could offer you a ride home in my carriage. The roads are treacherous this late and it has been raining for the past two hours, at least. Alone if that were preferable. My driver can return for me after dropping you home."

She didn't need to think about the offer. "No, thank you, my lord. I am quite used to being out in this sort of weather and at this time of night. Much of my work requires it of me."

"I don't expect anything in return." He grinned and altered the last statement. "No, I do. I'd like some of those little eclairs. I'll pay you for them, but I'd like you to make them for me."

"My lord, I can certainly provide you with the pastry. Gunters can supply you with any number of items, as you know." She couldn't help, but smile in return. He reminded her so much of a small child

146

wheedling for sweets. "However, I cannot return to my neighborhood in a carriage, alone or not, without causing speculation and gossip. Both would endanger my position at Gunters Tea Shop."

"Hmmm, that does not please me."

Without thinking, she asked, "And does, my lord, always get what, my lord, wants?"

That brought a silent moment and a bark of laughter. "I believe, I do."

Stepping back, he finally realized he had been blocking her in the pantry room. She grabbed her hooded cloak and curtsied, letting him know she was done speaking with him and was maintaining her independence.

Hunching her shoulders to the wind making its way between the tall apartment buildings and warehouses Michie peeked out the small opening she allowed in the hood she held closed with wet gloves. The walk was cold and miserable. Almost as miserable for the coachmen driving the cumbersome carriage behind her. They had been following her since her leaving Berkley Square.

It could snow soon or, at least, freeze the rain already on the ground making the pavers slipperier than they already were. She rethought her turning down the offer of the ride.

No, she had done what she had been taught. Do not accept favors. Do not make yourself dependent on others. There was only one other person in the world she cared about. To keep her safe, Michie must remain separate and secretive. She had lived through such storms before and she would again. She should focus on getting home to her mother and her bed.

The faded light at the end of her street finally

appeared through the gray of the rain and she exhaled the breath she had been holding. Safely home, again. She promised she wouldn't allow a gentleman's offer make her second-guess her priorities again. She heard the horses continue past as she unlocked the door.

Michie heard his voice before she saw him. She wiped her brow with the back of her forearm after staring into the hot oven. The light flaky pastry was sensitive and over-baking made it retain the bitter flavor of burnt wheat.

Glancing furtively, she saw the gentleman she now knew to be, Lord Hedley, and Gunter himself standing inside the kitchen. No one besides employees were ever allowed inside the inner sanctum of Gunters. Inside where new flavors of ices were tested and proved. Inside where flaky pastry is combined with creams and flans and sauces to make intriguing new confections.

Yet, there he was inside the room Michie always considered her safe haven. A place where she never had to worry about being caught out in a lie. A place that was a refuge from all she feared in the outside world. A place safe being what she was.

She busied herself with wiping off the stone-topped table to get ready for the hot pans. It was often used to make the molded candies, but those had been completed yesterday and there were no private orders at the moment. The stone would cool the pastry quickly and she would be able to fill them sooner. Allowing her to leave earlier than midnight for a change.

Peeking up to see where Gunter and his guest were heading so she could go the opposite direction, her gaze locked with the gentleman's. She knew he saw her, but didn't acknowledge her in the slightest. Perhaps he didn't recognize her wearing her baker's clothing rather than the uniform she wore to set up the pastries in a client's home. Perhaps it was merely a coincidence that this particular gentleman was in the same place she was. She eavesdropped on the conversation without guilt.

"I assure you, Gunter, I appreciate how well-equipped your kitchens are, but if you don't mind, I'd like to watch quietly. I find all of this…" The gentleman waved his hand to include the entire room although Michie felt his gaze stop on her a moment longer than anywhere else. "So very fascinating."

A front counter waiter came in and spoke quietly to Gunter who bowed to the gentleman and excused himself to handle something in the tea shop portion of the business.

Michie held her breath, but she could hear the gentleman make his way to her station. He stood there a moment in silence finally forcing her to acknowledge him.

"Please, my lord, do not tell me the only reason you are here is because I refused your escort last night."

"Not the only reason. I have a curiosity of the inner workings of a place such as this." She knew she hadn't rolled her eyes. Well, she thought she hadn't, but he continued, "I assure you I wish to know how everything is created. How wonderfully it is presented. I am sincere in my inquiry."

"Then I must excuse myself…."

"Oh, there you are, Lord Hedley." Gunter patted his rounded stomach which was a habit he had. "I see you found my best protégé. She would be a good one to answer your questions about the pastry and such.

149

Nothing goes on here that our Micheline hasn't had a hand in at one time or another."

She saw his lordship raise a brow in surprise. "Really? I find that very fortunate information in deed. I shall expect, ah, Micheline, to accompany any order I make from now on. I want only the best for my family and guests."

Bowing several times, Gunter expressed his delight. "Of, course, my lord. I wouldn't have it any other way. Micheline will be part of the delivery every time."

Michie could only seethe with resentment. Lord Hedley had known what he was doing from the beginning. Now she would never be allowed to escape going to Hedley House. Jumping with the sound of an oven-door clanking shut, she grabbed a dry cloth and tugged the giant door in front of her open. Moaning inwardly, she knew the puff pastry was too brown on top and tips. These would not have the light flaky feel or taste. And it was all that man's fault. He had distracted her and she forgot to pull the pans out.

She would need to remake them and try to find a time slot not already taken by something else needing to be baked in the ovens. Sleep was going to elude her again tonight. She wanted to rage, but that wasn't her way. Instead, she found a free table where she could mix the ingredients to begin again. Somehow, she knew Lord Hedley had left the kitchens and was once again in the front of the shop. She inhaled deeply then began her work.

The season was well on its way and Michie missed the free-time for experimenting with new flavors and styles. Tonight, she had made the light buttery puff-pastry into swans. Their wings up as they appeared floating on ponds. She nestled them into the paper dyed to appear as a stream with the savory filled swans floating across the table. The swans would be filled at the last minute and set in place. The full design required her to be at Southmont House hours before the event.

The entire table was to resemble a summer day in the country with small eclairs disguised as owls on a branch or log. She had created the Christmas favorite, *buche de Noel*, although it was weeks before that holiday. The chocolate frosting covering the cake looked so much like bark on a tree, Gunter had come over to investigate her work while she was creating it. To the side of each of the filled, rolled cakes she had put meringue mushrooms and jellied leaves flavored like spearmint sprinkled with large crystals of sugar.

The theme continued with pressed marzipan in shapes of fruits and nuts, along with real nut meats glazed and sugared with spices. Every mold, every confection was a story in itself and the waiters had come back with empty trays telling her how well the 'exhibit' as they called it was being enjoyed.

She placed the last of the meringue blue-birds into their nests made with coconut and frosting. Small candy eggs with liquid cream centers were under each one to be discovered later by the guest. These little surprises were her signature. Lord Hedley was in her good grace for allowing her free rein with the entire menu.

As if thinking of the man conjured him, she heard his voice call out to her.

"Micheline, I have someone who refused to wait a moment longer to meet the artist of the masterpiece in my dining room." He was guiding an elderly woman dressed in a beautiful gown from an earlier era. Her silver hair was in an ornate up-style supplemented by hair pieces, but unpowdered as it probably once had been when she went out in the evening.

"Madam Heroux, this is the young woman I have been telling you about. A *virtuosa* of the wire-whisk, pastry chef Micheline."

"Oh, my dear your idea was *magnifique*. Where did you get your inspiration? Your ability to detail is so wonderful. It made me yearn for the French countryside of my youth. I feel quite *la joie* seeing all the springtime when it is so cold and dreary here in England this time of year." The older lady waved her hands then clasped them to her breast, as she spoke in French. "And the *bouche de Noel*...to be used in that manner – pure genius. The taste took me back to France it was so true in spirit."

"I was taught the secret at a very young age, Madam. I broke many a cake until I learned the secret of using warm filling when I roll it. Then, it became easy."

Michie had answered the woman in French, a language she used only with her mother in the privacy of their home. She felt Madam Heroux would feel more comfortable, so continued allowing the older woman to enthuse about the various confections and reminiscence of her homeland – both their homeland.

The elderly lady tipped her head. "You remind me of another young woman. So full of life, so much joy. I liked her very much although we lost contact and then.... So many people were lost or became scattered. I hoped she was one of those who was saved." She tipped her head in another direction and said, still in French, "Although you have her mannerisms as well. Her laugh as I remember it."

Reverting to English, realizing she had allowed herself to go down a dangerous path, Michie glanced at Lord Hedley standing there with a speculative gleam in his eyes. "Oh, I must apologize, Lord Hedley, it has been years since I used my schoolroom French. Please forgive us for leaving you out of the conversation."

He smiled dividing his attention between the women. "No, it is quite all right. I understood much of the compliments Madam Heroux heaped upon your head. I must admit I became lost for a while when the words came so quickly."

Madam Heroux smiled and cackled. "We French are like that, you know. We speak with our lips, our hands, our shoulders. We can converse with one another without words, if need be."

"We must allow Micheline to return to her work, Madam. I see empty trays piling up."

"Of course. I simply wanted to give my compliments to the creator of such a delight. You will go far, my dear. I feel it in my bones – and these are very old bones so they know what they are saying." Another chuckle and she turned, as if painfully, and allowed Lord Hedley to lead her out.

Michie pushed aside the possible damage that had been done when she fell back to her native French, after years of making sure her words held no trace of an accent. She began filling trays with the last of the sugared biscuits made to look like flowers. Little bites of delight placed among the real, edible flowers painted with egg-white and sprinkled with sugar.

Worry about what Lord Hedley would think of her conversation with Madam Heroux was set aside. The exhilaration of knowing her creation had been accepted by the guests brought the excitement of the evening to a close. She couldn't regret meeting the lady. A lady Michie was sure her mother had met years earlier. Michie's main thought now was whether to tell her mother about the meeting or not. It was an unwritten rule never to mention their time in France nor how they came to be in London. That had been instilled in Michie since she was a child and knew it meant the safety and life of her mother if Michie ever forgot it.

Michie rode home in the small carriage alone. A driver and footman travelled on top in the drizzling rain, but she appreciated the transport after working into the late hours for the earl. He never mentioned his coming with her after the first evening when she walked rather than arrive home with him in a covered conveyance.

That night, she had bitten her lip all the way as the shadow of the large, crested carriage followed her through Cheapside's narrow streets. Feeling as if every window held multiple eyes watching and speculating. She had been glad to find her mother asleep on their bed when she finally made it into her apartment without other words passing between her and the earl.

Lord Hedley needed to take no for an answer or she would need to make herself heard. Perhaps make Gunter see that her going to Lord Hedley's house was not good for business. After the event's success, that may be difficult to do. She knew there would be an influx of orders from tonight's supper dance. She had heard too many compliments for there not to be.

Michie also knew those orders and compliments would increase the unease in the kitchen. Her name had been mentioned in the society columns as someone to seek out for new and fresh creations. That had been like a blow to the older, more experienced chefs. She found herself apologizing for her success and found the atmosphere strained even more when Gunter praised her for bringing new customers to his door.

Not that all this could be laid at Lord Hedley's feet. The earl had merely given her the chance to shine. To use whatever methods she wished to furnish suppers and buffets for his guests. He didn't even wish to approve the menu leaving it all up to her.

It was both a blessing and a penance. As one of the few females in the kitchens at Gunters, her workmates were not as generous in their praise. They did not wish to be compared with her in Gunter's eyes. Michie could do no less than her all – with design, food preparation and set-up of an event. And Michie's all was very impressive.

Perhaps her novelty would wear off and by the end of the year, she wouldn't be in such favor with the London hostesses.

Betty, the cook at Southmont House, was becoming a close friend. As close as anyone at Gunters since that kind woman wasn't in competition with Michie. "Just go on in, Micheline, dear. No one's about right now. They'll be returning when they take a break between sets or whatever they calls them things. I don't put my faith in playing cards, but I don't tell my betters what to do, either."

"I won't be long. I've most everything done. Simply need to decorate the trays and place the pastries."

"Did he order the plum filled meringues?" the round

woman asked, as if staring at the boxes Michie carried would tell her what was inside.

"Better than that. To assure you received one, I brought the damaged ones just for you. I'm training a new lad and he didn't realize how fragile they were. Kept crushing the sides when he lifted them from the sheets."

"Well, that's too bad for the lad, but sounds as if I'm going to profit from his mistakes."

"It happens. I used to find out what everything was by eating the failures the other bakers made."

She was getting used to Lord Hedley meandering into the room as she set-up. She was getting pretty good at ignoring him having explained the other times, in detail, what she was doing and why.

"I suppose you need to get back to the shop as soon as you finish?"

She hoped her mouth didn't fall open at the unexpected inquiry. "I, ah, I…."

"I probably should have started off by telling you, Gunter told me this is your half-day off. I know it was presumptuous of me, but you seem to escape or have a reason not to spend any time with me."

"My lord, we both know neither of us should be speaking like this to one another. We have already spent too much time in each other's company. If it ever became common knowledge…." Feeling emboldened, she said bluntly. "My lord, I could be fired." There, her fear out in the open. She had worked too hard to give up on her dream.

His smile felt tight as he bowed and left his little sugar-plum to finish her work. There was time, but for what? Michie had brought up very strategic points. What was he trying to accomplish by seeking her out every time he knew she was in his house? Any house?

Hostesses were becoming suspicious as he continued inquiring about the caterers they were using at their functions. Then to disappear into the back areas - past the green baize door. He had escaped notice so far since no one other than servants were there and none disposed to gossip about a guest.

His own home was different. He knew he had raised his cook's attention by being in a part of the house from which he was usually absent. One too many times he had gone into the kitchens to ask if the Gunter delivery had arrived, yet. My God, simply listing his bending of society's expectations, he questioned why everyone hadn't guessed his condition.

Was he ready to admit it to himself? The fact that he not only fantasized about the tempting morsels Michie brought him, but the fact he considered her one of them. Not bought and paid for like the rest, not something he could take with him into the library along with a cup of tea, not something he could sneak past his valet and enjoy in the privacy of his sleeping chamber. Not yet, at least.

He needed to get himself under control. Like any craving that grew too momentous, he had to stop. Stop ordering from Gunters. Stop yearning for the tempting tastes that filled his day with visions and his nights with dreams. Stop trying to fill a hunger that would only lead to Micheline's downfall.

CHAPTER THREE

After weeks of not ordering from Gunter's and driving past the tea shop even though it was out of his way, Cyrus broke his own rule. He found himself behind the green baize door of another hostess. Searching like a maniac for the small uniformed girl who held his heart as she held those damnable eclairs. He felt helpless to do anything besides continue in his quest.

The scent of vanilla and cinnamon led him to her. Empty boxes surrounded her while filled trays almost over-whelmed her as she placed each delicacy in its proper position.

"Lord Hedley, you should not be in here. I thought I made my feelings on the matter very clear."

"I am cognizant of your wishes. I only wish to see if you are still angry with me."

She seemed to be picking her words carefully. "I was never angry, my lord. Only, I know what happens to women of my station who become involved with gentlemen of yours." She held her hand up to stop his response. "No matter what your intention, it will become a problem for me. No matter how innocent the conversation."

"I could…"

"No, my lord, you couldn't."

A strident voice of his hostess interrupted anything more he and Micheline could have discussed. "Lord Hedley. How did you find your way into my pantry? I must assume you became lost on the way to the gentlemen's retiring room?"

"Just so, Lady Ashton. Your servant was about to give me directions, I believe, but as long as you are here…." He was hoping to take the woman out of Micheline's sphere. He put his arm out to escort his hostess.

"Sorry, my lord, I need to ensure myself that the preparations are proceeding as planned. I am sure one of the footmen can help you find the retiring room if you still find the need of one."

All he could do was keep from glancing in Micheline's direction. Instead, he bowed to the older lady and took himself away.

Damnation. What he feared the most had happened. He could only hope Lady Ashton wouldn't take her displeasure out on Micheline or worse, complain to Gunter about her. He would need to make some sort of reparation tomorrow. He would appeal to Gunter knowing Lady Ashton would not listen to his arguing of innocence for the hapless pastry baker.

He called for his carriage passing several arriving friends on his way out.

Michie felt cold - bone cold even in the kitchen still warm and smelling of cinnamon and other heavenly spices. Tonight, such scents didn't lift her spirits. Didn't entice her into making something excitingly delicious.

Tonight, she had been talked to as she had never been before. Scolded and called a name she hadn't heard except on the street of Cheapside. Lady Ashton had berated Michie for a full five minutes and then sent her away before the desserts had been trayed. Michie prayed that would be punishment enough for being found talking with a gentleman. A 'distinguished guest' as the lady had called him.

Michie hadn't pointed out that the so 'distinguished guest' had very pointedly come to where Michie was working not the other way around. Why were gentlemen allowed to do anything they wanted while poor working girls paid the price?

Slamming the bag of sugar down, she regretted her bad temper at once. She knew she would get into trouble speaking with the earl and she had continued doing so. She should have explained her problem to Gunter. Perhaps he would have stopped sending her to Southmont House or allowed others to do the setting up for a while. Why hadn't she forced the earl to leave her alone?

Measuring out the butter, she began blending the two ingredients. She knew why. She enjoyed speaking with Lord Hedley. Enjoyed sharing her love of baking and creating confections of all sorts. He always seemed so interested and he was always very complimentary of everything she created.

Was that why? Did she seek his approval and compliments? The attention he gave her as they spent time traying biscuits and comfits? Crystalized fruits and glazed nut meats? Was she so obvious that others saw her need? Was that why he returned over and over? Or why Lady Ashton was so angry when she found them together?

The sound of the backdoor closing brought her head up. Had she left it unlocked this late at night? A dangerous thing to do with so many people out of work and in need. Perhaps it was the driver returning to put away the ice although a glance at the clock told her he would have returned hours ago.

"Micheline?" She saw the hulk of him wearing his great coat enter her kitchen.

"Lord Hedley. I am busy and need to get these crème brulee into the water bath."

"The bath...."

"It does not pertain to anything, my lord. You must know what transpired tonight after you left. Lady Ashton sent me away. Now I will need to explain to Gunter how I may have lost him an account."

"I doubt she will do that. I happen to know her own staff is abysmal. She will need to get her midnight suppers somewhere." He smiled as if it were all a jest. "I will complain to all the ton how her edibles have dropped in quality if she stops using Gunter."

"My lord, that will not do and you know it. My reputation, Gunters' reputation, must be above reproach. If I survive this, I will need to watch myself very carefully." She gazed into his serious eyes. "We must never be seen alone again. And there will be those who will keep watch, I assure you. I am now a topic of gossip."

Leaning against the table, he said quietly, "You know that wasn't my intention."

Michie hated to ask what his intention was. She didn't want confirmation he had been talking her up sweet until he got his way. Until she met him in a less populated area where they could be alone. She glanced around them. Such as this kitchen in the middle of the night.

"Lord Hedley, I must ask you to leave this minute. Others are due back after the midnight suppers are finished. You cannot be found here, alone, with me."

"I agree. When are you done here?"

"I, ah, it will take another hour at least. But…."

"I will return. I will wait in back on the street. Come out and I will drive you home."

She tried to tell him that wouldn't do. He only firmed his lips.

"All right, but you must leave now. I cannot be distracted while I prepare these."

The grin she recognized as his playful one appeared. "So, you find me distracting?"

"I find you aggravating. I must finish these before morning so I agree to whatever will have you leave."

A flare in his sapphire eyes as he straightened taking a step away. Holding his hat in his hand he bowed his head while she ignored him. She had no more time to waste on the scoundrel no matter how attractive she found him.

Her heart sank at the sight of the crested carriage waiting, just as Lord Hedley said it would be. The weather was cold and a slight drizzle had the possibility of turning to snow given the chance. The footman that rode next to the coachman was standing by the door ready to help her in. She wasn't apprehensive entering the darkened carriage. For some reason, she knew she could trust the earl. Had trusted him from the beginning, if she were truthful with herself.

Settling against the soft squabs, Michie found herself encompassed by a warm body. Again, she felt no fear, but did prevent herself from snuggling her nose into his warmth. Breathing in the scent of sandalwood and cloves she closed her eyes. Tried to think what having this man near all the time would feel like.

Would she tire of this warmth? His smell? His concern for her comfort and happiness? For she did think he had been instrumental in her being allowed free rein lately to do as she wanted. Gunter had handed her more power than she had ever held before. She was certain it was due to the earl. Who else could have caused the change?

She felt the jerk of the carriage as it pulled into the empty street.

"Better now?" The voice she would never tire of hearing asked.

"Yes. I was warm from the kitchen, but that dissipated as soon as I walked outside."

"I believe it will be worse yet tonight."

"Don't you mean yet this morning? I believe we passed midnight long ago."

"Yet, you were still working."

"I actually prefer to have the kitchen to myself. I can take my time and not feel rushed by the others who need to use equipment or ovens. It is better to frost cakes when the kitchen cools down at night. I always do smaller batches of frosting. Not because it is easier beating it, but because it makes the frosting lighter. Breathes easier. I try to frost when the room is cooler so I return at night to work. I don't charge extra for the time."

"Is that because you don't feel you are worth it?"

The wheels drove over a hole probably caused by missing bricks. She bounced against his side. His arm tightened around her as she said, "We must be in Cheapside. I should have warned you the streets are not taken as care of here."

"You changed topics. I asked if you do not feel you are worth being paid extra."

"To be honest, I feel grateful for the opportunity to work at Gunters. To have people willing to train me. To have an employer willing to give me the chance to fashion new creations. I have begun calling them delights. Madam Heroux called them that and I liked the sound of the words. They differentiate what I do with the usual fare from Gunters. The pies and sponge cakes, biscuits and shortbreads. The items one can order in the tea shop."

"Delights." He seemed to draw the word out as if tasting it on his tongue. "I think I agree. What you do is so much more than placing biscuits on a tray. Even I could accomplish that with a little coaching."

"It is not as if all those things are not important, but they can be gotten so many places. I want to create something people will remember. That they will talk about even if the entire display is eaten by the end of the evening."

"Your ambition is admirable. You do realize it is taking a toll. You have very little time for yourself. You must have other interests."

"None I find as enticing, my lord." She sat straighter knowing she was getting closer to her home. More importantly, to distance herself from this man. A man who was amusing himself at the present, but could be so disastrous to any life she hoped to have.

"You were not calling me 'my lord' before. Why start again?"

"It is to remind me of my station, my lord. That I accepted your offer of a ride so we may have the privacy to speak openly. I admit we got off topic. Since I am almost home, I will say what I must." She knew she needed to be firm. Needed to leave him with no misunderstandings. This wasn't simply about her job. Even her life. She must make him see that his interference in her life placed her in an impossible position. "My Lord Hedley, although I appreciate your championing my craft, we can no longer meet as we have been doing. Anywhere. Ever. I do not need to list the reasons. You know them as well as I do."

He seemed to be mulling her words over. Would he fight her on this? She wasn't sure how strong she was against his attraction and appeal. Knowing something and being able to accomplish it were two different things.

"I agree although you must promise me you will still personally see to the catering of my annual Christmas celebration. So many of my usual guests are already asking me what it will be. I have gained quite the reputation for interesting as well as delicious suppers. I cannot disappoint."

"I am pleased and honored to design your Christmas party. I already have drawings of the plan and list of possible foods."

The carriage came to a stop and Michie knew she should leave. Step out and not look back. She felt this was a new relationship between the two. One she fought for, yet, still was disappointed she would no longer be able to talk with him as she used to.

"Thank you, my lord. I will be forever grateful for your sponsorship. It has not been unappreciated." Opening the door, the footman held her hand so she did not slip on the now slick pavers. She blinked rapidly hoping the man thought it was caused by the cold drizzle rather than the tears she knew they were.

CHAPTER FOUR

"Madam Chapelle, I would like a word with you, if you please." He urged her to listen to the proposition he had devised. "I am, Lord Hedley, Earl of Southmont."

"Monsieur, are we acquainted?" The petit woman wearing all black stopped on the sidewalk and turned toward him. He knew they had never met, yet she would give him the time to explain. Thank God she seemed more receptive than her daughter.

"No, although I am acquainted with your daughter, Micheline."

She said haughtily, "You call my daughter by her Christian name? How acquainted are the two of you?"

"Well, I think I know more about her than most, but much less than I wish to know in the future."

"Let me stop you here, my lord. I am not in the habit of acting as procurer for my daughter nor has she ever shown the propensity for accepting such an offer." Turning, she hurried her steps away from him.

Catching up with his longer strides, he tried to explain, "You misunderstand, Madam Chapelle. I have no ulterior motives for what I am offering you and your daughter."

A flash of dark eyes reminded her of his Micheline and met that gaze with quiet. He knew the two women shared more than their coloring.

"Monsieur, I am usually a modest woman. Do not mistake that for my not being passionate about certain things. One of those things is the safety of my daughter – by any means. You have my warning."

"I would expect nothing else. Your daughter told me much the same thing when I tried to explain my plans."

"You have already spoken to my daughter of these plans?" He nodded in acknowledgement so Madam Chapelle continued, "And she sent you about your day with a flea in your ear?" A smile spread across her face. So familiar yet different due to the years separating the two women.

"Very close to it, Madam. I was staking her future, my future, on your less emotional thinking. That you would know what was best for her."

She glanced both directions and nodded. "I will welcome your visit to my home in a few minutes. I take it you know where we live?"

Bowing, he expelled a deep sigh. "I do, Madam. I await your pleasure."

Tapping a knee with one hand, Cyrus waited with his usual impatience. If this plan didn't work out as he wished, would he continue his pursuit? Would he accept his dismissal as a woman's prerogative?

"Coachman, lead on." He rapped the top of the interior and sat back. Not that he could relax, but he needed to at least pretend to himself this was simply a visit to an émigré who needed his aid. Someone who did not hold his future and heart in her hand.

The carriage rocked to a stop outside the familiar, seedy looking house on a street of similar buildings. He dismounted without the step being lowered. Waving for his driver to wait for him, he knocked on the door he knew led to the upstairs rooms. The door he watched Micheline enter when he accompanied her home.

Madam Chapelle answered the door herself, emphasizing what Cyrus already knew. The two women lived in near destitution. Micheline not only worked because she wished to become a premier pastry chef, she worked to put food in her mother's mouth. Worked so diligently to keep her job while learning her craft. Following the woman up the stairs, he tried to ignore the signs of mold on the outer wall or the cooking odors coming from the downstairs apartments.

The two rooms seemed cramped, but were clean and well decorated. Items Madam Chapelle managed to bring with her from France? Possible family heirlooms? The Bow Street Runner hadn't been able to dig too deeply in the short time he had. It was enough for Cyrus to know he could offer Micheline more, offer Madam Chapelle more.

"Would you care for tea, Lord Hedley?" his hostess asked when they had sat.

"No, thank you. I wish to lay out my plan and, hopefully, gain your support."

Her smile was tight. "Then, please proceed."

"Perhaps I should begin at the beginning." He smiled, but the dark serious eyes merely watched him. She wasn't going to make this easy for him. The two ladies were very much alike. He hoped the older one would be more sensible.

Again, that Mona Lisa smile not telling him anything of her thoughts.

"I met your daughter when she was setting-up the wedding breakfast for my niece. It was being held in my town home. Micheline was having trouble dissuading a male guest of his pursuit. I sent the man on his way and apologized to your daughter for his boorish behavior.

"I became interested in what she was doing and grew intrigued over the whole process. So much so, I stayed and helped tray the convections."

The dark eyes did not soften. He was losing before he got to the point. "I did not stay with any forethought or plans. I was not there to coerce or compromise, I assure you."

"Yet, that is what happened." A statement not a question.

"Yes, but not then. Not in my home, but that of another peer. The hostess found us together." He hurried to explain the innocence of that meeting. "We were merely talking and, in fact, your daughter was trying to get me to leave. I wanted to stay a while longer…."

"Why was that, my lord? You know society's rules. How impossible a match between you and my daughter would be."

"I, ah, I do. That is why I began my search into her French connections. Many émigrés come from perfectly acceptable families. I was trying to find a reason for us, for me and Micheline, to be more to one another."

Standing abruptly, Madam Chapelle said sharply, "I believe you have over-stayed your welcome, my lord. I will see you out."

He stood, as well, not able to ignore etiquette. Putting out his hand in supplication, he pleaded, "Madam Chapelle, I implore you. I love your daughter and I need the ammunition to make her see a relationship, a marriage, is not impossible between us."

She sat quickly, as if her legs had weakened and let her drop to the seat recently vacated. "Monsieur, if that is truly why you are here then you have a solid ally. I have always believed my daughter lost more than a homeland when we had to escape France and all that was happening there."

"It is the only reason I have intruded on your privacy. I know there are many reasons for people to leave France. But I have not had time to research your story. I was hoping you would tell me. I could perhaps find a way for Micheline and me to be together. For her to accept the position she would have as my wife."

Bending her head, he could see the slight woman pat her eyes with the plain hankie pulled from her sleeve. "I have wanted only the best for Michie. She was so small when we had to grab only what we were wearing and run. My old nursemaid's nephew, a fisherman on the coast, brought us across the channel. We made our way to London hoping to hide among the many. At the time, there was chaos in many areas." She seemed to be remembering another time. "No one knowing what would happen. Who would be sent back for trials? For illegal acts against the people. Then Napoleon.... It has never stopped. Never returned to normal."

"So, is there anything you can tell me to help my persuading Michie, you called her? I like that."

"A pet name. A name her father gave her before he was sent to prison. I continued to use it to help her remember him. He doted on her and she was devastated when he simply disappeared. I feared she would be next so I made plans. I sold everything I had to pay for papers to leave Paris, to take her to a safe place."

"Did no one help? I thought there were groups of men, an underground of other aristocrats who helped people escape."

"There were, but I was not so lucky." She stood and strode to the other side of the room which was not all that far away. He let her tell what and how she wanted. For some reason he knew this was the whole reason Madam

Chapelle and Michie had remained out of sight and alone instead of joining the other émigré who were in the same boat, so to speak.

She never turned to face him and he felt she was reliving the time she fled her homeland. "I was not married to Michie's father. Not that we did not live as if we were, but Rene was already married. When he was quite young, his family made a marriage pact between him and a neighbor. They had no children between them and he was already forty when we met. I lived with him for years. There were those who thought we were wed we had been together for so long. Then I had, Michie. No one could love a daughter more than, Rene. We had a wonderful life together – for a while."

Cyrus didn't need to hear about the anarchy and subsequent carnage among the French aristocracy. The thousands of lives, both noble and not, lost to the guillotine as well as the sword. No, he could only thank God and this woman Michie had been saved. Now he needed to save her again and place her where she belonged. Among the noble families of the ton.

He needed to bring the woman back to the present. Finding a way, he and Michie could be together. "I am sorry for dredging up these bad memories."

Turning to him, he could tell she had been crying. "There were good memories, as well. I haven't thought of Rene in many years. I find the pain lessened and the happy times worth reviewing. I should tell Michie more about her father."

"I believe I have the information I was seeking."

"There is more that I need for you to know. I am wanted for killing a man."

"When? How? Here, in England?" How was he

going to get around this? How to make Michie understand they should be together even if it brought to light a crime her mother committed. Was still wanted for.

"We were packed, what little we could carry. A man, a revolutionary tried to prevent me from taking Michie. Said she was her father's daughter and should face the same fate. I couldn't let him take her. She would be killed as so many others had been." Shaking her head furiously, he saw the passion that fueled this woman into doing what she had to. What freed her and Michie from the claws of the revolutionaries.

"Do you know his name? Perhaps the file has been lost. Perhaps no one is looking for you any longer?"

"In my prayers, I have wished that to be true. But I used my husband's sword and sliced the man in half. So much blood…. There will be no leniency for me, I am sure."

"There must be a way to free Michie to marry me and keep you protected. My name would go a long way once your daughter is my wife."

"I would never stand in Michie's way to become a countess. She was born into the aristocracy. I am but a daughter of a mere French Sire."

"But considered noble. Are any of your family left? Will they vouch for your honesty? That you killed this man to protect your daughter?"

Shrugging, she shook her head slowly. "Non, no one is left that I know of any longer. They were gone before I moved in with Rene. I knew no one would prevent me from doing so. No one cared either way."

"I must think on this, Madam Chapelle. I appreciate you entrusting this information to me. I promise, I will be very select with whom I share it."

Again shrugging, she returned to the chair and sat. "If my exposure allows Michie to live the life she should have had, then I will accept my fate. Others with less guilt have met a much worse end than a French prison."

"I will show myself out, Madam. Sit here and rest for I fear this has all been more strain on you than I thought it would be."

Taking the stairs quickly, Cyrus searched his mind for anyone who could help him in his quest. Now that he knew who Michie was, he had to free her to marry him. Free her of the guilt he knew she carried as much as her mother did.

CHAPTER FIVE

Michie hurried up the stairs to her home. She didn't have much time before needing to return to Gunters Tea Shop and travel with the order to the Smyth home. It didn't need to be laid-out before eleven so Michie had taken the opportunity to visit her mother during the day. A luxury and she had brought desserts as well as the famous savories Gunters provided.

Pushing the door open, she called out, "Maman, I have a surprise for you."

Michie stopped as she realized her mother wasn't alone. And the woman accompanying her mother was not their landlady collecting the rent. Instead, Madam Heroux sat across from her mother with a pot of tea between them. Catching herself in time, Michie apologized for her hasty entrance.

"Madam Heroux, how nice to see you again." She bent to kiss her mother's cheek and to assess if she were upset by the elderly woman's visit.

Her mother smiled, saying, "It must be very chilly outside. Your lips are quite cold." Patting the seat next to her on their short sofa, she continued, "Come join us for tea."

"I will, of course, Maman. Let me plate these first." She stepped to the sink counter and pulled down their prettiest plate from the shelf. Setting the numerous macarons and savories in a pleasing pattern, she returned to her mother's side.

Madam Heroux spoke first as she peered at the offerings placed in front of them. "Your mother and I were speaking of our youth." The elderly woman chuckled, "Well, her youth. I have many years on her, but was very active back then. So many parties and dances. Balls that would last till four in the morning." She selected a macaron and bit into the cake-like sweet filled with chocolate ganache. "These are so good I feel as if I were in my Aunt Charlotte's sitting room. Her chef used to make these for the young people to nibble after dinner."

Maman surprised Michie by chuckling in response. "My mother's chef would let us raid his pantry in the evening. My older brother found that if he left a bottle of cognac, the secret remained within the kitchens. It was such fun – enjoying our pilfered treasure in the upstairs sleeping chamber."

It was the first time Michie knew of an older brother, an uncle Michie knew nothing about. She would remain quiet and possibly learn more of her mother's early life than ever before.

Her mother poured more tea to their visitor. Madam Heroux said, "Oh, Jeanine, do you remember, Monsieur Vaux? The dance master? My daughters were students and fell under his spell immediately. My husband had him escorted off the premises after he found him, um, dancing with our oldest son without benefit of music."

Michie's mother replied, "Oh, really? I had such a crush on him. I was heartbroken when I heard he left Versailles. I had not been old enough to take lessons, yet, so I was forlorn at missing the opportunity."

Madam Heroux shrugged her shoulders. "He really was a handsome young man, but perhaps not enough of a man. I am sure he landed on his feet, like a cat. He never seemed short of admirers and patrons." She sipped the freshly poured tea.

Michie thought about what was being discussed and decided the dance master must have been one of those men who danced in Molly houses. Men who felt most comfortable in the presence of other men.

Her mother confided, "By the time I was old enough, my father had lost his money and my brother was dead from a duel. My whole life changed, it seemed as if in a trice."

Her mother seemed so lost and alone at that moment. Michie thought perhaps this meeting wasn't such a good idea after all. But then her mother laughed as better memories pushed the sad ones out.

Jeanine told them, "Oh, I do remember being at a lawn party. A sort of Venetian breakfast. They had brought in sheep and other bucolic animals for atmosphere. They had let loose dozens of *lapin*, rabbits, to hop among the diners." Another laugh escaped as she must have remembered more of the event. "The young boys let the hunting dogs out. They said later it was to play with them, but when those dogs saw all those rabbits – oh, my, what chaos."

"I was there that day, too, *ma cheri*. My chair was tipped over by those uncontrolled hounds. My shoes ruined." Madam Heroux tut-tutted about the lost footwear.

Michie's mother concurred to the misery. "I know, my dress was torn, but I was laughing so hard. And hoping the bunnies escaped without harm. I did not wish to see the poor frightened things hurt. I am sure the boys regretted their actions later."

"I am sure, as well. One of those boys would have been the future king, but that would not preclude him receiving a whipping." Madam Heroux said with a shrug, "I miss those days. Simpler times to spend with friends."

"Yes, my time ended sooner than some others." Looking over at Michie, her mother added, "Not that I regret anything today. I would change nothing."

Michie knew her mother meant meeting Michie's father. Of living with a married man openly and bearing his child.

Madam Heroux said, "*Ma cheri*, you must come for tea at my home. It will be nothing as ornate as that Venetian breakfast of years ago, but there will be excellent tea and good fellowship. Please say you will join us? Others you may know. Others still trying to put their lives back together. We all have a different way of viewing things now. You will be most welcome, I assure you."

Michie was waiting for her mother to give one of many excuses she had used in the past. She was startled when her mother said, "I would love to, of course, *mon ami*. I will look forward to doing so."

Michie was still thinking about her mother's abrupt change of policy when Madam Heroux rose saying her farewells. Michie stood, as well, as her mother walked with the elderly lady to the front door.

Her mother returned and seemed somehow younger. Younger and more alive than she had been in a very long time. "Those were lovely delights, Michie. I am so glad you chose today to bring home some extras."

"I'm glad as well, Maman, although I think Madam Heroux enjoyed your talk just as much. I wasn't sure what to do when I heard her Parisian accent. I couldn't ask her when she left the city. Did she tell you we met one evening at Southmont House?"

177

"Yes, once we began talking." Tipping her head to the side, her mother replied, "I was surprised to see her at the door, of course, but recognized her immediately. Suddenly, I wished to speak my own language with another. Remember things I thought I had forgotten completely."

"I am glad. Truly glad for you, Maman. When you visit her, make sure you take a hackney. I don't wish you to tire yourself walking a long way."

An odd expression crossed her mother's face. "I do not think it will seem like such a long way, *ma cheri*. I think it will be like returning home."

Mishie tried to stand tall, but at her petit stature that wasn't much. This would be the first time she had arrived at Southmont by way of the front door. All the other times she had come through the kitchen and remained, for the most part, behind the baize door.

She had to climb both steps to reach the brass knocker giving it two lifts then waiting patiently as the lady she was. The butler, whom she knew, opened the door to her without question. Evidently Lady Talbot had told the staff Michie was expected.

She shifted the pages of designs and menu possibilities from one hand to the other nervously.

"Right this way." The butler walked rigidly to an area Michie had never seen before. Too far from the dining rooms and room used for the midnight suppers to be familiar territory.

She openly admired the soft green of the parlor she was left in and the darker green brocade furniture. She found the soft yellow tones of the carpets and white painted woodwork relaxing. This must be a room the family used often in the evenings when they were at home.

The blue brocade dress she wore was appropriate for such a room. For the business woman she considered herself. Not too severe, but certainly not making her appear to be aping her betters. The hat sported two dyed feathers tucked into the wide band. She had removed her gloves and left them with her cloak in the foyer. It hadn't been hung-up so she assumed that meant this was to be a brief meeting. She hoped she would get the information she needed before being sent on her way.

The double doors snapped open and Lord Hedley stepped in closing them behind him. Was she to work with his lordship as well, then? Not really a problem as long as he agreed with his sister. She did not want to act a buffer between the two if they were at odds with how they wished their Christmas party to be presented. She knew Lady Talbot had liked the wedding breakfast, but the designs Michie held in her hands presently were more to his lordship's tastes.

Standing quickly, Michie curtsied which felt strange. She realized she hadn't curtsied to the man as often as she should have. "Lord Hedley, is Lady Talbot not here, yet?"

"Lady Talbot will not be attending. To be honest, she knows nothing of this meeting. I wished to get time alone with you so we may get things straight between us. Come to an understanding."

Danger bells clanged loudly in her ears as she measured the distance from where she stood to the door so many steps away. "Ah, my lord, I thought we came to a conclusion days ago. Nothing has changed so I must insist you allow me to leave."

"I will not come closer than I am right now." His expression was one of hurt. "Do you feel unsafe in my presence?"

"No, never unsafe. I merely feel it very unwise. If I am to work with your staff, they cannot think it has to do with some, let us say, unsavory agreement between the two of us."

His brows came down as he frowned at the idea. "I would fire anyone who thought so on the spot."

"Ensuring everyone else would think the same, as well." She shook her head. "I cannot allow myself or Gunters' reputation to be placed in such a position."

"We are getting off point here, Michie. I want us to have an understanding."

"Michie, you called me, Michie? Why?"

"That is part of what we must discuss. Evidently your mother did not tell you of our meeting." He must have received his answer by her shocked expression. "We had a long conversation of what was possibly keeping you at arm's length. I discovered you were protecting your mother. I can honestly say, Madam Chapelle is in no danger at all."

"Then you don't know the whole of it. She is in danger of the hangman's noose, if not worse, if she is discovered to still be alive."

"I have men seeking information about the man in question and what the authorities may have. So much from that time period has been lost when government buildings burned and officials replaced. The Napoleonic controlled government is not much better. But the men I have on it will bring me what there is."

"I don't think anything you can do will change what happened. I have heard her cry in her sleep. When I wake her, she refuses to tell me about it. I know she is reliving that night. The night we escaped from Paris."

Lord Hedley sat next to her on the sofa and took her hands in his. "Michie, I promise you. I will not rest until your mother is safe and secure here in England. That nothing from her past, nothing from France, will be a danger to her life or happiness."

The door came open and Lady Talbot stood there taking in the two sitting closely on the sofa. To his credit, Lord Hedley did not jump to his feet or try to distance himself. Michie felt he remained to give her support if she needed it. After seeing the flash of anger in his sister's eyes, Michie felt she needed it.

The lady asked, "Lord Hedley, may I have a word with you in another room, please?"

Sighing he answered, "No, Margaret, you may not. If you have something you wish to say to me, you can say it in front of my fiancée."

"Your what?" If Lady Talbot hadn't screeched the words, Michie was certain she would have.

He ordered his sister, "Stop sounding like a fish-wife. Close your mouth and sit down over here."

Lady Talbot obeyed, although Michie thought out of reflex rather than knowingly.

"Cyrus, you cannot mean to…. ah, to…."

"When, dear sister, have I ever said anything I did not mean? This isn't some drug induced state, I assure you, although I find Michie headier than any liquor or opiate." He peered at her reaction. She wasn't impressed. He would need to work on his technique, if he thought this was the way to Michie's heart.

"Michie?" Lady Talbot stared from one to the other on the sofa seemingly unable to tell which was going to evaporate into thin air first. The baroness was unable to understand anything at the moment. Weakly the lady asked, "Isn't she the, um, with the caterer?"

"She is much more than that, but we'll discuss that at another time. I simply need you to understand Michie and I will be married as soon as we have completed the Christmas season. I do not plan to share my bride with a group of hostesses clamoring for special desserts and designs for their New Year's Eve celebrations."

Michie tried to dislodge her hand from his while hissing, "My lord, you do me a great honor, but I find I must decline for reasons I have already explained to you."

He gazed into her eyes steadily. "And I have explained how your reasons are not legitimate. They simply do not pertain to the two of us."

"I disagree. If there were any two people who do not belong together, it is you and me. I have no standing, no linage, no place in your world. I work as a servant."

"I will concede you have very good arguments. I am not ignorant of the difficulties that will arise between us, but I feel we can conquer them with time and patience."

Michie wanted nothing more than to end this speculative conversation between the two of them while Lady Talbot looked on with great interest.

She tried to appeal to that lady. "Lady Talbot, I came under the impression I would be speaking with you about your family Christmas party. I have some ideas, but this is a very personal celebration. I wish to have your thoughts and ideas incorporated into the design."

It was as if that woman woke from a spell and finally walked toward the chair opposite the sofa upon which Michie still sat. Michie slid away from Lord Hedley while he watched her. She half-expected him to draw her back into a conversation. She hadn't capitulated to his wishes and she knew he hadn't given up – on anything.

To begin as she meant to when she arrived, she asked, "I understand this has been an annual event for you? What things do you remember best about the previous ones? Any traditions you wish to keep as part of this year's celebration?"

She asked this of Lady Talbot, but it was Lord Hedley who answered. "Wassel. I remember the first time Mother allowed me to imbibe. It made me feel as if I had gained adulthood although I was only twelve."

Lady Talbot added, "And eggnog. I love it and we only have it once or twice a year."

Michie wrote the two beverages to her list although she was thinking of using them in a much different manner. Possibly molded ices set in bowls of crushed ice. She continued to write as the siblings added more memories of the decades of holiday fare and games.

"I have enough for now. I thank you both." Michie gathered her pages of notes and drawings. "I will have some final drawings to show you, Lady Talbot, within a few days. I already have Gunters' kitchen booked so it comes down to the final meal selections."

Lady Talbot shot her brother a warning glare before leaving the room.

Lord Hedley had stood when the ladies had. Now he blocked Michie's path to the door as he said, "I look forward to our next meeting, then."

"As you wish, my lord. You are the customer and your wish is my command."

Michie saw the flare of passion in his eyes before he bowed over her bare hand and kissed it, his lips warm upon her skin.

"I am much more than that to you even if you refuse to accept it. I will keep working toward that end." His gaze was intense as she made her way around him.

Cyrus put out his arm and caught Michie around the waist. He turned her into him, allowing their bodies to align. "No, you don't, my sugar plum. We need to speak to one another and not about business."

"We have nothing besides business to discuss, my lord." She sounded so prim and proper, and prim and proper thoughts were far from his mind.

He pulled her onto his lap as he lowered himself to the sofa. "At one time, I would have agreed. That was before I knew my own heart. Now, all I can think about is when can I convince you we belong together? When can I have all of you?"

"The cook who taught me much of what I know, told me to take all compliments with a grain of salt. It brings out the honesty."

"I am being honest…"

"I know. The salt was from my tears. I knew we could never be what you wanted. I can never live as my mother did with my father."

"You remember him? How old were you when…he was taken?" He wasn't sure he wanted to speak of this now. Perhaps it was for the best, so she wouldn't feel she was coming into this marriage with secrets.

"I was six. I can't remember exactly when my father had been arrested. Maman was trying to keep me from knowing how much danger we were in. I didn't figure it out for years afterward. I did not ask because I know what Maman had to do to save us."

He held her tighter to him. Allowed her to tell him what he already knew. Had Michie actually seen her mother cut the man down? Had she witnessed such a gruesome death at such a young age?

"I ran back into the house to fetch my special pillow father had given me. It had a picture of Versailles painted on it and I had always slept with it."

Her breathing had increased and he wished he could take some of this painful memory from her. Be her strength.

"I stopped as I got to the parlor door. Maman threw down a bloodied sword to the floor. I could see a body crumpled in front of her. Her wide skirts covered most of him, but I knew he was dead. Even that young, I knew."

"Did your mother see you?"

"No, I think she was in shock. Anyway, that is what I felt later, whenever I thought of that day as I grew up."

"You thought of it often?" Again, an ache in his heart for what he couldn't protect her from. How much worse it must have been for her mother to live with such a thing.

"I think I pushed it out of my mind as a child. Later, I thought of it as more of a nightmare. I remember traveling in some sort of cart pulled by a donkey. It was full of empty bags that smelled of soil and vegetables. My nurse was with us and a man who owned the cart. My nurse's brother from the country, I think. He took us to an abandoned sheep shed where we stayed. I don't know how long, but I remember being hungry. I remember my nurse leaving then retuning with raw potatoes and carrots which we ate as they were. Later someone else came and we were taken by a different cart to a port along the coast. Nurse was not a good sailor, so Maman and I stayed on deck facing into the wind. She said it would keep me from getting ill. I always thought it was some sort of magical potion only she knew. Not simply the wind in our face helping ward off *mal de mer*."

He thought he heard humor in these memories. Perhaps they all weren't bad. That Michie only had memories best forgotten.

"Maman made sure I remembered my father. He was always a very good father. Indulgent to the point of spoiling me although I think he was simply that kind of man. Liked to indulge both my mother and me. Perhaps to make up for the fact I was only his natural child."

"Do not think that makes you less of anything. There are more natural children among the ton than anyone realizes. It is not the stigma it once may have been."

"I understand. Although, I do not think I will ever consider myself in any other manner."

"And I never will." He had to make her aware of his feelings on the matter. "For some marriages, especially those made for political reasons, are often replaced by another bonded with love. I think your parents was one of those. Your father chose to live with you and your mother in defiance of convention. It tells me much about the man and his principles."

She gazed into his eyes and smiled. "I like that you liked my father. I do not know anyone else who knew him."

"Perhaps one day we will. Madam Heroux, for example. She knew everyone who was anyone."

"Yes, perhaps you are correct. I should visit her with Maman someday."

"We will visit. All of us together. You are not the only one gaining a family and history. We shall discover yours. I think your mother will be more open to sharing her life, as well. She will be free to do so without worry of consequences."

He kissed Michie wishing they could go upstairs and really get to know one another. Instead, he let her stand. As she straightened her skirts, he reminded her. "You are probably running late to someone's event. I will await our next meeting with bated breath."

He enjoyed the blush on her face after their light love making.

She managed a dignified curtsy and rushed out while he composed himself to meet with his sister, whom he thought would still be there. He was not going to escape so easily, he knew.

CHAPTER SIX

"I assure you, Madam Chapelle, there are no charges pending against you for anything."

The woman dressed in widow black, bit her thumb nail. "But I killed a man. In my parlor as I was trying to escape with Michie. Her father had already been imprisoned as had his wife and family. I knew they would come for us, or at least, Michie. I could not allow that to happen."

Cyrus could tell the woman was becoming upset with the memories and the old fears she had lived with so long. He could not envision what it must have been like for a young mother alone in a city that had gone mad. Unimaginable things happening daily.

Leaning over, he clasped her hands between his own. They felt small like Michie's did. "Madam, you are safe now. My men were very thorough in their search."

"How can that be?"

"The man you said you killed had been deemed an enemy of the state only that day. There was a warrant for his arrest. He would have been put to death along with others who were sentenced for embezzling funds thought to belong to the state. Men who lined their pockets with bribes and stolen wealth from the beginning of the tyranny. Many found themselves hanging on the gallows or beneath the blade of the guillotine."

"You are certain?" she asked before shaking her head. "Of course, you are certain. I have never met a man so focused on what he wants. On what he desires."

He didn't pretend not to understand. This woman

had known from his first visit his desire for her daughter. The reason he was helping her achieve freedom from the fears of the past. The fears he had now assured were in the past and nothing to fear again.

She smiled with the sheen of tears in her eyes looking much like Michie did when she cried. "I cannot thank you enough. I have been imprisoned for over a decade by my fear of being found out. In doing so, I limited Michie's life, as well. I wouldn't have anything to do with the French émigré here. Not until Madam Heroux visited and told me I would be more than accepted into their group. I have met with her twice now and find such comfort. I didn't know I was so lonely. I have made Michie as fearful. As wary of people."

"Leave Michie to me, madam. I will make sure she is well taken care of."

"I have much to be grateful to you, my lord, but I will not allow you to harm my Michie. I lived that life and it almost killed me. I cannot condone anything like that for her."

Had the woman forgotten his promise to her before? That he would never bring harm to her daughter? That he loved Michie?

"You can tell as much or as little to your daughter, although I feel it only right that I tell you I plan on making her my countess."

Her smile and relief were rewarding. "I feared you had changed your mind since she is still working. I thought, perhaps, you had come to another agreement. She isn't the same lately. Sadder, I think, although she doesn't tell me anything. It is merely a mother's instinct."

"She is worried about what will happen to you if

people begin to wonder about my wife. Where she came from. My sister and family members will act as a buffer, although I have no worries. She has an acceptable pedigree with your family, alone. Her father – he was who he was and again, isn't a barrier."

"But she works, has earned her livelihood."

He knew he smiled widely. "I see her more as an artist. A creator of beauty. Food for the body as well as the soul. Her designs nourish the imagination. She makes me think every time I see another of her creations."

"She is all of that. Although I have never seen what she does at these midnight suppers and balls."

"You will at Southmont House on Christmas Eve. It is to be quite the extravaganza."

"I could not come to your home, my lord. I will have Michie tell me all about it, though."

"No, I insist you attend. I will send my coach for you and you will stay the evening as a guest in my home. The next day, your new house on Curzon Street should be ready."

"My new…oh, my lord, I cannot accept such generosity."

"As my future mother-in-law, I feel obligated to make sure you are well cared for. I know you would wish to keep your independence. Be able to entertain your new friends freely. I have opened accounts for both you and Michie at several dressmakers and shops my sister uses. I will send a list. I encourage you to visit them soon to get your Christmas clothes."

She clasped his hand. "I don't know how to thank you."

"Talk your daughter into accepting my ring. She still hasn't said she would be mine. I am not sure of her decision."

"I think you have won her heart, but she is not one to trust easily. Too many years of peering around corners for revolutionaries seeking revenge."

"I don't plan on letting her push me away. Perhaps she will realize she is free. You are both free. I want her to choose me. Not see me as an obligation."

"Ah, *ma cheri*, that is not a problem. I hope she is her mother's daughter and goes with her heart. She will never regret that choice."

Nervously Cyrus paced the carpet in the same parlor they had met Michie in before.

"Will you sit, Cyrus. She will be here. If anything, your Micheline has proven herself a professional. There is only a week to finalize the plan so she can't put off meeting with us any longer that I can see."

Smiling, he said, "I know, sister dear, but I am hoping she will give me her answer today, as well. I have done everything in my power to convince her I am trustworthy. That I do as I say. That I care about what she cares about."

"If she is foolish enough to toss such a man as yourself over, then there is no help for her."

Chuckling, he answered, "Said like a prideful older sister. If I have not won her heart, I will send you to argue in my favor."

The light tap on the door as the butler ushered in Michie brought the conversation between siblings to a halt.

Michie curtsied, but he sensed subdued excitement. She wore the same blue dress with feather hat as she had the last time. So, she hadn't taken advantage of the

191

accounts he set up. Did she even know of them?

She walked across to the tea table and set out some sheets of paper. "My lady. My lord. I think you will be very happy with my designs."

He and his sister moved to see the drawings together.

"Oh, Micheline, these are fantastic. Please explain them so I know exactly what each part is," Margaret said peering over the sheets.

With a bare hand, Michie pointed daintily to a pastel colored drawing. "I took what you said and put it to paper. Picture everything on pristine white. The linen, the napkins and the stands holding the food. Or possibly crystal. I want the table to sparkle like new snow on a sunny day or the stars in the night sky." She was practically sparkling as he watched. "As you can see, the colors you thought of for the season are all here. The oranges you found each Christmas morning will be used in several items. Welcoming pineapples, hot spiced cider, and foods easily eaten while walking around or standing. Long tables separate the diners too much. If guests can mingle, they will be free to talk to those they wish to speak to and not only the ones on either side of them. Keeping that in mind, I developed the entire presentation to accommodate mingling and movement."

Michie peered up to see how her words had been met. He knew he was intrigued and glancing at his sister, he could tell she was as well.

Michie continued, "I have Wassel flavored ices, orange frosted petit four using sugared orange peel as garnish and orange crème puffs. Lady Talbot, you mentioned cherries. I have devised a method of covering the maraschino cherry with a liquor-flavored fondant and then encapsulating it all in a hard chocolate shell. These will be set among the plates of biscuits and other petit fours…."

Margaret couldn't withhold a groan. "Oh, I can almost taste them now."

"Soon, my lady, but I feel they need this week to mature, like fruit cakes and brandy." She seemed pleased at Margaret's reaction. "Speaking of fruit cakes, there will be traditional Christmas puddings, small personalized size dribbled with flavored frosting. Pineapple shaped marzipan, candied almonds, sugar and spiced walnuts tossed about the trays. As if left by angels like gifts from the Magi."

Still sounding excited, Margaret said, "Explain these dangling snowflakes."

"They are a type of melted sugar drizzled on cloth, allowed to set then sprinkled with crystals of sugar so they sparkle. I will hang them from a sheer line between the chandeliers above the table. They will hang at various heights for guests to pick out of the air."

"Oh, how charming. Like picking stars from the sky." Margaret couldn't stop her words of admiration. Nothing made him prouder than to see the two women in his life getting along.

He spotted something he thought he knew, but needed to ask. "These cloud-like items. What are they?"

"The meringue filled with various fruit sauces. I call them sugar plum fairies and will be set on crystal plates so they appear to be floating."

Margaret sighed, "You are so creative, Micheline, it is difficult to imagine the time and effort going into these things."

"That was the dessert portion. The entire list will be

given to you," Michie explained while sliding a sheet under the others revealing one done in pencil.

Cyrus chuckled, "The desserts are the only part that ever interests me." He received almost identical sighs of exasperation from the ladies.

"This is the food line as I envision it. Again, staying with the flavors you both felt the holiday exemplified. There will be chilled duck *l'orange*, crab cakes with a pepper-pineapple glaze, smoked capon, cheeses, aspic, chilled asparagus, and orange glazed carrots. Most are tried and true to Gunters so I am sure you will find them acceptable. Again, there is a complete list for you."

Margaret said with a sigh, "Micheline, I cannot imagine what you do. The time to devise recipes let alone figure out all the ingredients as well as where to find them."

He took Micheline's hand before she could gather the sheets together and make her escape. "Come, sit with me, Michie. I have missed you so much."

Margaret glanced at him and he met her gaze steadily as she said, "I will trust you, brother, to behave and not compromise our guest. I would love to have her in the family, but it must be on her terms. I do not believe she will accept anything less."

His sister hurried from the room leaving the two of them sitting quietly side by side, watching the fire as it burned low in the fireplace.

Trying to remain proper and remind her they had things to work out, Cyrus began. "I have missed you, terribly."

"I have been busy, my lord. This is the last weeks of the season before parliament takes their holiday break. Gunters, therefore I, are stretched to fill the orders. You were lucky you had this one scheduled so early. We have had to turn down several others already."

"I took that into consideration. That is one reason I haven't been visiting Gunters' kitchen at night or following you around the entertainments I am sure you were setting up."

Remembering he wanted to be honest with her at all times, he added, "And I wasn't sure I would not pressure you for more."

"My lord…" Definitely a warning.

Changing tactics, he asked, "Has your mother spoken to you about her plans?"

"Certainly, and I appreciate everything you did to make that happen. To give her the freedom to live again. She carried that fear for too many years."

"I might not have done so if I did not care so deeply for her daughter." Thinking better of it, he said, "Not that I expect that to sway you. No, that's not exactly true. I want you to look on me as a friend and protector and a man in love. I helped your mother because I felt it would help you. Free you to become my wife."

"But what of my career?"

Cyrus thought her words boded well for his plans. She was, at least, thinking of the future and what his thoughts were on the matter. This is where he must not make a mistake. "I was hoping you would see yourself as more of the grand master. In a manner, orchestrating the events, possibly meeting with hostesses to design a plan, but leaving the actual baking and decorating to others. Give the newer pastry bakers a chance."

He had been holding her hand the entire time they had sat there. She gazed into his eyes and he hoped she could see his love and desire. She continued staring up and he lowered his head taking her lips to his. She tasted sweet, as she always did, but this time she hadn't been eating confections. This time, he realized, it was all her. Her scent, her firm lips, her taste.

Pushing himself back from her before he became carried away with passion, he took a moment to catch his breath. Keeping his hands to himself, he said, "I don't mind sharing you. Not if you come home to me. I will take whatever time you can spare for me and be grateful."

There was a sheen of tears in her eyes. "I don't think you deserve the leavings. You have given me so much. I can only see you satisfied with all or nothing. Right now, I am torn between two loves and it is breaking my heart."

He kissed her several more times before groaning with frustration as he helped her leave the warm confines of his arms. "Go, my little sugar plum. I need to think rationally for a while."

As if realizing how much time had passed, Michie rushed from the room.

Cyrus could only sit and stare into the fire praying she hadn't just made up her mind.

His Christmas party guests were still talking and imbibing. The amount of food was beginning to thin – finally. The tables had actually been groaning from the weight of the delicacies and platers of substantial meats and offerings. Cyrus knew the demand on Michie was over for the night – demand as a Gunters' employee, at least.

He had seen Michie come into this room, a library used by Margaret for writing letters. He searched the shadows for the shape of her dress. The white one set with rhinestones he had ordered and had delivered to her apartment. He had hoped her mother could talk Michie into wearing it, which she had. And Michie had allowed others to keep the trays full while she accepted the well-deserved compliments of his family and guests. She made a gracious hostess and no one questioned her right to be on this side of the baize door.

Finding her in the corner, he told her, "Michie, you are not escaping into the kitchen or butler's pantry or where ever else you seem to get to."

"My lord, this is inappropriate. I came to escape the noise and heat. I shouldn't even be in here."

"This is exactly where I want you. Where I need you." His mouth covered hers and she quieted, accepting his salute.

When she was able, she whispered, "My lord…"

"Say my name. I know you know it."

"I do, my lord, but I should not do so. We are so far apart in station. I should not even be here."

He grinned. "I believe we have gone over that already. This is where I say, 'this is where I want you'. Where the woman I love should be. Where the woman I plan to marry should be."

"Cyrus, you cannot keep saying these things. They make my heart want to burst with pride to be your chosen countess, but you know it cannot happen. We are too far apart…"

Why did it always come down to this? How could he make her see she was an acceptable match for him? As a French émigré, she would be forgiven a more plebeian life here in London.

"You are your mother's daughter. A daughter of a marquis."

"A daughter of a marquis, but not of his marchioness. My mother has no birthright to claim. I have no father's name. After the Revolution, not even a family."

"It is enough to give you credence, if you need to justify our passion, our love. Me? I do not care. I love you with all my heart. I have desired you more than the addicting convections you entice me with."

Startled by those words, she denied them. "I did not entice or lure you. I did not do any such thing and you know it. You could have gotten any of those items from Gunters at most any time."

"But not from your fingertips. They always tasted better knowing you touched them."

"Cyrus, what am I to do?"

"You won't need to do anything. We will introduce your mother into society, move her onto Curzon Street into a house I have already purchased."

"Why do you have a house on Curzon Street?"

"I will explain that at another time. Possibly months after our wedding when you will understand my motivations. For now, it is quite a proper address for an émigré. You will move in with your mother for the few days until our wedding."

"Cyrus, Cyrus, I can't simply take from you…."

"You will give me much more, my sugar plum, believe me. You will ease my soul, you will return my love, you will give me children. I never before thought of having a wife, not even to beget an heir. Now, that's all I can think of – begetting children."

He ignored the sounds of guests leaving, hearing the muffled voices grow farther and farther away as people made their way back to the main parlor for more music.

The singing of Christmas carols and drinking of Wassel and warm eggnog.

Sighing deeply, he urged Michie to the short sofa and pulled her onto his lap. She curled against his arm facing up. "Michie, please put me out of my misery. Accept your fate and tell me you love me. At least half as much as I love you."

"Only half, my lord?"

The humor he heard in her voice gave him hope. After all she wasn't a cruel person. Not one to say things to hurt another. "Half would be more than I deserve, I am sure. I have made these past few months difficult for you."

"Yes, you have…but also wonderous. I found a whole new world because of you. I would still be frosting petit fours in the middle of the night if you had not championed me, freed my artistic expressions."

"I would have done so regardless, but love got in the way. Made what I assumed was to be a simple patron of an artist into much more. It didn't lessen your freedom although it did complicate things. I caused others to doubt your talent and I am sorry for that."

"Gunter never did. What others said I put down to jealousy. There is always a certain amount of drama in a bakery. Artistic temperaments clash. You should hear the wars that go on when we are selecting new ice flavors – or who has rights to naming them."

"One thing I must insist upon. You will not make your own wedding cake. It can be simple. It can be as high as the ceiling. It can be anything as long as someone else makes it for you."

She pulled his head down to reach her lips and they kissed. Not long enough for Cyrus, but he knew she had accepted him. Had agreed they would be married and soon. His heart beat so loudly he thought she would hear it. Would know how much she affected him.

"Oh, Cyrus, how I do love you."

"Yes, I know. I knew it from the moment I saw you covered in fairy dust sparkling in your hair and on your cheeks."

Chuckling, she nestled closer. "That was crystalized sugar and you know it."

Snuggling her closer, he whispered, "I didn't dare chance a taste of you right then. Later I did and found you the sweetest confection of all."

"I will always treasure the first time we met. I think I fell a little in love as I watched you eat that éclair."

"Hmmm, I believe I did, too."

A word about the author...

A voracious reader her whole life, author Susan Payne loved the written word. When reading more than fifty books per month wasn't enough, she decided to allow her mind to take flight and write all the many stories that kept intruding into her life. She blended her love of history and her love of words to create over eighty stories. All historical and centering on a couple finding love and a happy ever after together.

You may contact Susan at:
http://www.authorsusanpayne.com or
authorspayne@gmail.com

Thank you for purchasing
this publication of The Wild Rose Press, Inc.

For questions or more information
contact us at
info@thewildrosepress.com.

The Wild Rose Press, Inc.
www.thewildrosepress.com